Scottish
Bakehouse
Mysteries™

A Faerie
Dangerous Game

Rachael O. Phillips

Annie's®

AnniesFiction.com

Books in the Scottish Bakehouse Mysteries series

Library of Congress-in-Publication Data
A Faerie Dangerous Game / by Rachael O. Phillips
p. cm.
I. Title
2020935353

AnniesFiction.com
(800) 282-6643
Scottish Bakehouse Mysteries™
Series Creator: Shari Lohner
Series Editor: Elizabeth Morrissey
Cover Illustrator: Kelley McMorris

10 11 12 13 14 | Printed in China | 9 8 7 6 5 4 3 2 1

"**K**eep quiet, you two! You're going to get us caught," Carol MacCallan ordered her friends through gritted teeth. Although retired from teaching high school math, she could still call upon her commanding schoolmarm voice whenever needed—even when the audience was her former college roommates, who were now her business partners.

Molly Ferris, hunkering her petite frame behind a big pine's scratchy trunk, merely rolled her eyes, but Laura Donovan tossed her auburn head. "Yes, Mrs. MacCallan, oh great and mighty math instructor, Queen of Calculus—"

"Hush." From the midnight darkness of their forested hiding place, Carol aimed an ear at a nearby Classical Revival-style home. "Do you want Hamish to hear us?"

Laura quieted immediately. The three women may have employed retired history teacher Hamish Bruce at Bread on Arrival—the Scottish bakehouse they ran together in Michigan's Upper Peninsula—but the prickly older man could nail all three to the wall with a single curmudgeonly glare.

Playing a so-called "faerie prank" on him would bring sweet revenge. Or certain doom. And what better time than this, the Month of the Faeries? The Loch Mallaig tradition was celebrated every October, and the town's residents always went all out with their lighthearted hijinks.

A single light shone on Hamish's front porch, and a night-light in the shadowy kitchen cast a dim glow. Carol, watching the upper story, adjusted the overfilled trash bag in her hand. "Good. He just turned off their bedroom light."

Before Carol could finish the sentence, Laura slipped past her, zipping through the night quickly despite the bulky load she carried over her shoulder. Tossing their own bags over their shoulders, Carol and Molly followed her to Hamish's shed, skirting his cherished garden to reach their second hiding place.

Carol didn't have to see well to know the shed bore not even a speck of dirt on its perfectly painted surface. In the flashlight's dim beam, she could make out the silhouetted symmetry of sculpted bushes and areas where patches of rich, jewel-colored chrysanthemums surrounded artistic displays of hay bales, cornstalks, and pumpkins. Hamish and his wife, Joyce, had worked hard to create this pretty autumn scene.

Carol readjusted the heavy bag she carried over her shoulder, memories of long-ago student pranks testing her resolve. Should they really spoil such loveliness simply to follow a silly local tradition?

"Yes." Laura had read Carol's fidgety mind and fingers. "Yes, we should."

Molly shifted her bag. "Let's do this."

"But I hate to mess up Joyce's yard." Carol and the others adored Hamish's patient, cheerful wife.

Laura smirked. "She'll enjoy his reaction enough to forgive us."

She sure will. The thought of the verbal fireworks their prank would elicit fueled Carol's resolve again. "You're right. Where do we begin?"

"We can start in the center of the yard, then each work our way in a different direction," Molly said. "Laura, you go left. Carol, you go right. I'll cover the center moving toward the house, then we'll meet at the shed. Just don't go near Nessie." She nodded toward the garage that housed Hamish's pristine green 1955 Studebaker Speedster. "That's something we'd *never* be forgiven for."

"Roger that," Laura said.

After moving to the start point, each woman set down her plastic bag and untied the knot at the top, then reached in and pulled out a handful of cubed bread, grinning wickedly at each other once they were armed.

"I thought Hamish might catch on when we didn't contribute much to the day-olds shelf, but I don't think he noticed," Molly said.

"He'll certainly notice this," Carol replied. "Ready?"

"On three," Laura said. "One, two, three!"

With dramatic gestures, the three women tossed their bread wide in three different directions, then got down to the task of spreading their cubes across the entire lawn. Once she completed a section, Carol toted her bulky sack a few more feet to the right, occasionally stealing glances at the house to make sure neither of the Bruces were peering out the window. As she went, warm wickedness bubbled up, similar to the feeling she'd had so long ago when playing a similar prank on the yard of her unsympathetic driver's ed teacher.

Hurry, Carol chastised herself. No time for memory lane right now—or for imagining Hamish's utter shock when he glanced out his window while brewing his morning tea and saw hundreds—maybe thousands?—of geese, ducks, wrens, robins, warblers, and sparrows on his lawn. The avid bird-watcher was used to tracking down his subjects in parks and along hiking trails. *What a surprise it will be for the birds to pay Hamish a visit this time.*

Carol smothered chuckles as she quickly completed her task, then headed for the shed to rendezvous with the others.

Molly had finished first and gone to fetch the pinnacle of their efforts from her Honda Fit, which was hidden on a dirt road in the neighboring forest. She held the small, bulky item in her hands. "I'm glad we took pictures of our masterpiece. Who knows what Hamish will do when he sees it?" she whispered to Carol once they were reunited. "Want to see the result of all our hard work?"

Molly fixed her own small flashlight on their creation. Though Carol knew perfectly well what to expect, she winced slightly as a multimedia replica of Hamish's disapproving face emerged from the darkness.

Molly giggled. "You really nailed it with the idea of using a neep as a base, Carol."

Instead of a pumpkin, Carol had suggested they go with the traditional Scottish vegetable—which resembled an enormous rutabaga—for their jack-o'-lantern inspired caricature. Complete with craft-store sparrows and robins tangled in a beard of fake white hair, it bore an uncanny resemblance to their cantankerous friend.

Joining them to fix an appraising eye on the decorated vegetable, Laura nodded approvingly. "The birds are a nice touch."

"He'll hate it," Carol said.

"He'll love it," Molly countered.

"The best kind of prank," Laura said smugly as she turned off her flashlight. "Now who's going to put it on his front porch?"

Silence.

Carol frowned. *Oh come on. We can't back down now.* Her husband, Harvey, had tried to talk them out of the prank. But if they chickened out at this point, he'd never let them forget it—especially her.

"We came up with this idea together," Carol said, straightening her spine. "And we should finish it together."

"That'll increase our chances of getting caught," Molly warned.

"So what if he does catch us?" Laura challenged. "Will he shoot us at dawn?"

Certainly not, but Hamish could make their life . . . interesting. Carol repressed a shudder, imagining how their sharp-witted friend would retaliate.

Renewed silence told her the others shared her scary imaginings.

Carol shook off her reservations. "Let's do this. We'll sneak onto the far side of the porch, away from the light—"

"Let's put Hamish Junior on the porch swing." Glee had returned to Molly's voice. "You know Senior drinks his tea there almost every morning."

"Can we ring the doorbell?" Laura framed her thought in a question, but her tone left no doubt what she would do.

"If you drag Joyce out of bed, it's on your head," Carol warned.

"Nah," Laura said airily. "She'll make Hamish check it out."

Carol peeked at her watch. "Whatever we do, let's make it fast. We need to get *some* sleep before another early morning at the bakehouse."

They circled toward the front yard, Laura carrying the neep and Carol leading the way. Apparently, her careful pace wasn't fast enough. The other two slammed into her from behind, nearly knocking the trio off their collective feet.

"Oof!" Carol tried to steady herself.

"Sorry, but Laura ran into me." Molly's whisper echoed in the darkness.

"I thought we were trying to hurry," Laura growled.

"Is Hamish Junior okay?" Carol asked.

"Loosened one bird's claw when I slipped, but all good otherwise." Laura's exaggerated yawn hinted that she wanted to speed up this operation.

Carol set off again, tiptoeing closer to the front porch. Her caution apparently amused her friends, as barely suppressed giggles bubbled up from Molly and Laura. A smile twitched on Carol's own lips, and it soon blossomed into a full-blown grin. When a laugh threatened to erupt, however, Carol pressed her lips together. Shoulders shaking, she tried to smother her mirth, but that only increased her partners' amusement.

They staggered onto the porch, and Laura set the neep down on the swing. The glare Hamish Junior fixed on them only intensified their merriment. Hand planted firmly over her mouth, Carol stumbled down the steps, leaning on a near-hysterical Molly as Laura hit the doorbell.

Its echoing *ding-dong* cleared Carol's head, and she dashed for the woods, Molly sprinting behind her. At the sound of an opening door and an accompanying roar of wrath, though, Laura passed them both.

The giggles attacked again as all three took flying leaps across a small stream and dove into a scratchy thicket for cover.

Flattened on the cold, moist ground, Carol asked herself if their nighttime raid was worth it. *Oh, most definitely.*

Listening to Hamish's indignant—and fortunately incoherent—tirade before he slammed the door, Carol nestled in the sheer joy of having scored one for their side.

Maybe they'd drop in on Hamish next October too.

Too few hours later, as she dragged her fiftysomething body to the bakehouse in the still-dark early morning, Carol wasn't so sure.

Neither were her partners. For the first hour or so, they spoke in monosyllables and moved in slow motion.

"Why'd we ever listen to you, Carol?" Grouchy Laura dumped flour for apple cinnamon rolls into their giant mixing bowl.

"Yeah, why?" Molly, setting out pie plates, eyed her too.

"Excuse me?" Carol, up to her elbows in cookie dough, raised an eyebrow. "If I recall correctly, this was a group idea. A prank that would carry on the noble tradition of Month of the Faeries."

"But you were the one who came up with the midnight breading idea," Molly retorted. "Highly out of character for you, I might add."

"And yet you both agreed." Carol scooped another ball of dough out of the bowl and plopped it on her baking sheet. "Besides, you two were the ones behind Hamish Junior. I merely suggested the neep as a proper medium." A sudden grin tickled her tired mouth. "I can't believe we pulled it off. Junior was a perfect likeness."

A chorus of chuckles brightened the kitchen.

They faded when Molly asked, "Do you think Hamish has seen him up close yet?"

At the sound of a key turning in the back door, Carol grimaced. "I imagine we'll know soon."

Sure enough, feet stamping on the floor mat and a familiar harrumph echoed in the hallway.

"Maybe he won't suspect us," Molly whispered, ever the optimist.

Laura snorted.

Carol exchanged glances with her partners as their handyman entered the kitchen. Hamish simply studied them in complete silence, his steel-blue eyes piercing them. Carol thought she heard Molly gulp.

Finally, he spoke. "My, you're all looking a bit weary this morning. Perhaps sleep escaped you last night? I've heard Month of the Faeries can cause group insomnia."

Laura kneaded bread dough in silence, focusing as if it would disappear if unsupervised. Molly suddenly seemed overly engrossed in a spreadsheet where she tracked online orders.

Hamish waited.

Carol, realizing she was shifting from foot to foot like a guilty child, forced a smile. "As a matter of fact, I am a little tired today." She yawned for effect as she filled the cookie press with dough. "But I'll catch up on my sleep tonight."

"A good idea. Going to bed early is key to good health." Hamish leaned over Carol's workstation and added, "Though it can be difficult to sleep with a troubled conscience."

"Yes, I-I suppose it can." With him so close she could smell his aftershave, Carol scooped cookies like a machine.

"Because we all reap what we sow." He shifted his gaze to Molly and Laura. "Do we not?" Hamish turned and strode out of the kitchen. A faint, menacing chuckle echoed from the hallway.

For a moment, no one moved.

"Gee, I wonder if he knew it was us," Laura said drily, then glanced at the wall calendar and groaned. "It's only the third of October."

"Maybe we should have waited until closer to All Saints' Day," Molly fretted. "It wouldn't have given him as much time to retaliate."

All pranks had to cease by the first of November, which began a week of good deeds called the Seven Days of Kindness.

"It's a little late to think of that." Carol slowly shook her head. "We're dead."

Weary after the previous night's shenanigans and a busy day at the bakehouse, Carol nailed her husband with a suspicious glare. "You didn't tell Hamish that we were planning to prank him, did you?"

"Of course I didn't." Harvey, who was stirring spicy pulled pork in their kitchen's slow cooker, met her scrutiny without flinching. "He's on to you, eh?"

Carol sighed. She should have known that Harvey, a retired investigative journalist, would be able to keep a secret. "With a whole town full of his former students and disgruntled fellow citizens, you'd think Hamish would find someone else to focus his suspicions on. But he seems to assume we're to blame."

"Which you are." Harvey pointed his big spoon at Carol. "I told you that targeting Hamish wasn't a good idea." He grinned. "Better you than me on the wrong side of any pranks Hamish might pull. I wouldn't trade places with you for anything in the world."

"Thanks for your support," Carol retorted. Considering Harvey had fixed them dinner, however, Carol decided she'd overlook her husband's gibes.

Harvey encircled her with his strong arms. "Sit down and put your feet up while I finish the salad. It's your own fault that you're so tired, but I still can't find it in my heart to make you do anything."

A few minutes' rest and the delicious supper restored Carol's sense of perspective. She and her partners had spent entirely too much time today wondering how Hamish would repay them. Of course, he'd added to their angst as he worked around the bakehouse with uncharacteristic good humor, occasionally materializing behind them wearing a smile and holding a loaf of bread but saying nothing at all.

Brushing away the image, Carol finished loading the dishwasher, then dropped onto the cushy sofa in front of their log home's fireplace. Harvey sat beside her, and together they savored the crackling fire's warmth.

"It won't be too long until we'll need a bigger fire than this. Cold weather will be here before we know it." Harvey wiggled an eyebrow at her. "Bet you'd love to go ice fishing with me."

"You know better than that." She shivered just thinking about venturing out on frozen Loch Mallaig, the town's namesake lake.

"Ah, come on." Harvey shot her his most charming grin. "A real Yooper doesn't mind the cold."

"Maybe I haven't lived in the UP long enough." *Not that I'll* ever *have lived here long enough to go ice fishing.*

But Carol heard the note of wistfulness coloring her husband's voice. The bakehouse had kept Carol and her partners busy during summer tourist season. Throw in their involvement solving some recent mysteries in town, and she and Harvey hadn't had much fun together lately. And, after all, they'd moved from Pittsburgh to Loch Mallaig not only to be closer to their 33-year-old daughter, Jenny, and her family, but also to reconnect with each other after retiring from their respective demanding careers.

She slid her gaze sideways toward Harvey. "Maybe we could go fishing before there's ice involved."

"How about tomorrow?"

Harvey asked the question so smoothly, her wifely instincts shouted what she should have realized from the start: he'd set her up. "All that talk about ice fishing! You were just conning me into going tomorrow."

"Please?" After decades of marriage, he still could melt her with his expert puppy eyes. "You've been working too hard and need rest. Besides, you've only gone fishing with me a handful of times this year."

She really didn't like to miss church, the grandkids might want to come over, and her house to-do list was a mile long. And yet . . .

Carol squeezed his hand. "Of course we can."

"Great." Harvey tugged her to her feet. "We'd better go to bed now. I'm setting the alarm for six."

"Better than my usual time," Carol said with a chuckle.

As they snuggled under the colorful quilt spread over their rustic pine bed, Carol savored the view through the French doors that led to a small, private deck. Stars glowed like miniature lanterns in the dark sky, and the evergreens' spiky tops were silhouetted against the crescent moon.

Tomorrow, brisk breezes would clear her head as she and Harvey drifted in his little boat in the clear, blue water. Tranquil bays lined with scarlet, golden, and russet hardwoods, set against the richness of dark green pines, would ease her tensions. Perhaps they'd catch a few fat lake trout that Harvey would grill for supper.

Carol's mouth watered as she settled her head into the softness of

her pillow. Maybe Harvey was right. A little fishing trip might be just
what she needed.

When Harvey's alarm went off the next morning, Carol groaned
and covered her head with a pillow.

Harvey tugged warm covers from her grasp. "Come on, honey.
Time to get up."

She clung to her pillow for a moment, then relented. Grumbling
under her breath, Carol stretched like her indignant cat, Pascal, then
pulled on her oldest jeans and flannel shirt.

As she stumbled into the kitchen, the fragrance of sizzling bacon
and fluffy pancakes rewarded her reluctant cooperation.

Harvey smiled at her as he flipped a pancake. "We'll have fun
today. I promise."

Carol still wasn't sure of that, but when it came to bacon—plus
Harvey's winning smile—she was an easy sell.

A short while later, bellies full and brains invigorated by the crisp
fall air, she and Harvey carried fishing poles and other gear, plus a big
thermos of strong coffee, down the short, forested path that led to
their dock.

Gilded rose streaks painted the eastern sky and reflected in the
lake's glassy surface, confirming that she'd made the right choice.
Carol breathed in the morning's escalating beauty. Maples, like giant
bouquets of red and orange, contrasted with creamy white birches and
their shimmering, golden leaves. As the sun rose, dark pines, hemlocks,
and spruces glowed as if made of green velvet. Harvey's fishing boat
bobbed a gentle welcome as Carol, a seasoned fishing partner, stepped
into its bow.

Fishing didn't excite her like it did Harvey, but she was beginning to believe today would be a special day, a memory they wouldn't forget—Carol froze.

Then she screamed loud enough to wake the entire town in time for church.

2

Harvey grabbed Carol's hand. "Honey, what's wrong? Are you okay?" She could only point.

Harvey followed her shaking finger and gasped.

A large rattlesnake, coiled to strike, watched them from behind the middle seat, eyes glittering.

"Don't move," Harvey choked out.

As if I can. Carol hadn't realized rattlers sometimes appeared in Michigan's UP until she'd moved to the woods and been warned to watch out for the reclusive but deadly Eastern massasauga rattlesnake. She'd barely given it a second thought—before now, when fear paralyzed her.

Still, she knew better than to think Harvey would rescue her. Her journalist husband, who had intrepidly investigated everything from corporate corruption to the mob, feared snakes like nothing else.

"Back away, Harvey," she murmured. "Call animal control."

"Animal control?" Harvey still hadn't regained his breath. "It's Sunday morning and we're in the woods. It'd take forever to get ahold of anybody. Besides, I forgot my cell phone." He inhaled a shaky breath. "And I won't leave you with that—that thing. Not for a minute."

Loyalty was nice, but . . . Carol slowly reached into her coat pocket and pulled out her phone. The boat wobbled a little.

The snake didn't stir, its eyes still locked on her.

She didn't dare fiddle with searching for animal control's number, yet she couldn't bring herself to call 911. Maybe Yoopers considered rattlesnakes in boats everyday occurrences. Carol tried to calm her still spastic heartbeat. Jenny and her husband, Craig, had lived here for years. Maybe Craig would know what to do.

Carol willed her hand to hit speed dial. Her fingers fumbled at the phone's screen.

Then the phone slipped from her grip.

Thump. It smacked the bottom of the boat.

Harvey grabbed Carol's hand and yanked her from the boat. It dipped up and down.

The snake still hadn't moved an inch.

Carol's eyes narrowed. *Wait a minute...*

"When you stopped by the bakehouse yesterday, did you happen to tell Hamish you hoped to take me fishing today?" she asked Harvey.

Recognition dawned in Harvey's eyes as he slowly nodded.

Carol grabbed an oar and poked the motionless reptile. Instead of striking, it flopped harmlessly in the bottom of the boat.

"Rubber," Harvey said bitterly. "But realistic."

Very realistic. Hamish, a champion of good quality, employed only the best in everything he did.

Carol's flash of anger faded. Now that she didn't fear for their lives, she supposed she may as well chuckle. "I guess we started this."

"What do you mean *we*?" Harvey demanded.

"You're right." She joined him on the dock and dropped a light kiss on his cheek. "Since I'm responsible, I'll take our little friend here up to the back porch. Maybe he'll come in handy for some future Month of the Faeries prank."

"Nope." Harvey shook his head vehemently. "That thing's going into the trash can. Along with any more ideas you may have about pranking *anybody*."

"All right." Carol humored him, though as she retrieved the snake, she couldn't help wiggling its head at him a little.

"You want to end up in the drink?" he growled.

Spoilsport. She deposited the snake in the trash as promised, then kept an eye on Harvey in case he decided to make good on his threat.

As they glided out into the lake, though, Harvey's mood improved. They caught trout so small they had to throw them back, so he took her to local Scottish restaurant Neeps and Tatties for an early lunch. Carol and Harvey paused at the dining room entrance, inhaling mouth-watering fragrances while they waited to be seated in the cheerful, crowded restaurant.

While they were standing near the hostess stand, a sudden commotion broke out in the dining room. A rail-thin, raven-haired woman wearing a cropped jean jacket had stood up from her chair and was raising her voice at Brodie McCauley, the restaurant's owner.

"I don't care what you say, those sausages were inedible and I'm not paying for them!" she shouted, glaring with heavily-lined blue eyes.

"Ma'am, I—" Brodie began, his raised eyebrows nearly meeting his mop of thick, red hair.

"Matter of fact, I'm not paying for anything," she went on. "At this rate, I'm likely to get food poisoning." The woman threw her napkin on the table and grabbed a trendy backpack better suited to someone half her age. As she stalked away, the pointed toe of her high-heeled boot caught on the leg of another customer's chair, and she stumbled slightly. Righting herself, she strode out of the room, past Carol and Harvey, and through the restaurant's heavy wooden front door.

"My goodness," Harvey murmured to Carol. "I've never heard a bad review of this place."

"There's nothing wrong with our food," Brodie reassured the MacCallans as he approached the host stand. Brodie and his wife, Scotland native and professional chef Catriona McCauley, shared cooking duties in the restaurant they'd opened after Brodie had retired from his career as a Chicago firefighter.

"I've never eaten a meal here that I didn't love," Carol said.

"Better get you some breakfast, then." Brodie grabbed two menus and led Carol and Harvey to the far end of the room. He pointed to a table by a window. "Is this all right?"

Carol, who loved pleasant views away from the kitchen, said, "It's perf—"

Harvey stiffened and elbowed her.

Hamish, sitting with Joyce at a nearby table, wore a smile so big his face could hardly hold it. "Well, and how are you this fine Sunday? Any luck fishing?"

"Not a lot." Harvey hastily sat in the chair facing away from Hamish.

Say something. Carol opened her mouth, but where was the funny, biting response she longed to throw at Hamish?

Meanwhile, Joyce aimed a sharp glance at her husband.

Hamish appeared not to feel it. "It's a shame the fish weren't interested. Maybe you should have baited them with bread." He shook his head. "You know, I have found that a Saturday excursion, rather than Sunday, brings better results. Perhaps if you hadn't missed church this morning..."

Carol dropped into her chair and grabbed her glass of ice water. She hoped the cool drink might put out the heat flaming in her cheeks.

By the next morning, Harvey, who didn't hold grudges, had laughed about their fake-snake encounter.

Carol savored the relief that now flowed through her. She no longer had to fear Hamish's retaliation for her part in the night raid on his property. His sense of justice had been satisfied—at least where Carol was concerned.

Making the usual predawn drive to Bread on Arrival, Carol pondered whether she'd tell Molly and Laura about Hamish's revenge—and wondered what devilment he'd designed for her partners. But did she really want to know?

Fumbling for the bakehouse's back door key, Carol steered her thoughts toward her to-do list for the morning.

As she opened the door, a scream of agony sent her dashing to the kitchen, where Laura was screeching like a siren.

Carol did a quick scan of the room. No scary intruder. No blood.

"What's wrong, Laura?" Carol put an arm around her hysterical friend.

Molly, with mascara on only one set of eyelashes, burst in seconds later and added her attempts to console Laura as she continued her tirade.

Growing more and more concerned, Carol shot a puzzled glance at Molly. Had there been an emergency in Laura's family? Perhaps her father, Kirk, had had a heart attack. Maybe her teen niece, Adina, had been in an accident. But their friend seemed more angry than fearful.

Carol grasped both of Laura's hands. "You have to tell us what happened."

Eyes boiling in tears, Laura finally gasped, "He—he—oh, how could he do this?"

"Who? Do what?" Molly demanded.

Words failed Laura again. She could only point to the door of the storeroom.

Now that Laura had quieted, Carol aimed an ear toward the door. Was something lapping water?

Molly had already reached the doorway. She perched hands on her slim hips. "Angus, what are you doing here?"

Her lovable Scottie barely acknowledged her presence, greedily licking what appeared to be cream from a lovely pink dish with crimped edges. It was Laura's favorite porcelain tart pan.

Uh-oh. Carol cringed.

Though she eagerly shared her cooking knowledge, Laura was less generous with her hallowed personal cookware. She wouldn't loan it to anyone, even Carol or Molly. Both knew that a few items—including this delicately flowered tart pan Laura had treasured since before her years working as a chef in New York City—had been at the heart of her biggest culinary successes. She swore these special dishes and utensils possessed an almost magical quality that elevated her cuisine above others.

They were not to be touched by anyone else. For any reason.

Red-faced, Molly grabbed her pet and hauled him away from the dish. Licking the last creamy drops from his whiskers, Angus eyed her with reproach.

"Laura, I'm so, so sorry," Molly squeaked out helplessly.

"It's—it's not your fault." Laura blew her nose on the tissue Carol handed her. "Certainly not poor Angus's fault." She straightened, brown eyes snapping. "I don't have to guess who's behind this."

Carol decided to say nothing. If they wanted to accomplish anything today, she'd better wait to mention Hamish's prank on her and Harvey.

Molly remained silent too as Laura gently picked up her tart dish, murmuring comfort as if it were an injured kitten. She disinfected the dish several times before immersing it in a soapy bath, where, Carol figured, it would soak for a whole day—at least.

They had finally begun mixing, kneading, and baking the day's offerings when Hamish arrived.

Rarely talkative during early hours, Hamish wished them a

jaunty good morning. Carol and Molly muttered replies, then buried themselves in cake decorating and cookie cutting.

Laura was removing steaming cinnamon chip scones from a baking sheet when he entered. At the sight of him, she slammed the tray of scones on the counter and folded her arms.

He met the chef's dagger gaze with an innocent one. "Where's Angus?"

"Molly took him upstairs." Carol moved between Hamish and Laura. "He might have gone out his doggie door to the yard by now. Why?"

"I brought him a treat." Hamish held up one of Angus's favorites.

Even Laura couldn't help staring. Though Hamish claimed to dislike Angus, he sometimes sneaked the dog biscuits. Still, he never actually admitted it outright.

Today, however, he waved the treat like a small banner. "Angus is a good dog, you know. He does *exactly* what you tell him."

As if anticipating Laura's next move, Hamish ducked out of the kitchen.

The spatula she hurled never touched him.

———————————— ❧ ————————————

A day later, Hamish was still messing with their heads.

"I wonder what he's planning for me." Molly winced as she and Carol arranged Scottish breads on trays in the glass cases. After Laura's traumatic experience the previous morning, Carol had fessed up about Hamish's snake prank, and Molly was now quite on edge. "Do you think he's saved his best—well, worst—trick?"

"Don't let him get to you," Carol advised, though she tried not to imagine what he had in store for her friend. "Maybe he's decided not to prank you at all."

Molly raised an eyebrow at her. "Are we talking about the same Hamish?"

Carol gave her a rueful grin. "Good point."

Fortunately, they'd kept busy this morning, with lines of customers at the counters. Carol looked up to see Prilla Dunn enter as she had every Tuesday since Bread on Arrival opened. As usual, the tall, sturdily made woman walked as if she were in her sixties instead of around forty.

Though her hair was a pretty shade of blonde and her features were quite pleasant, everything else about Prilla—drab coat, out-of-date clothes, and heavy men's boots—seemed musty with age. She wasn't uncommunicative, but her voice was quiet and flat, and she never smiled.

Somewhere inside that emptiness, though, a spark of creativity must live. Carol had seen samples of woodburning art Prilla had created in Thistle and That, the gift shop next door owned by Doreen Giobsan. Doreen said the small, detailed pictures of birds, squirrels, and other forest creatures sold well, and the trinket boxes bearing Celtic designs were a huge hit with tourists.

Despite her demeanor, Prilla had drawn Carol's attention from the beginning. She wasn't sure why. Perhaps Prilla resembled someone she'd known a long time ago, but Carol hadn't been able to figure out who it was.

Now, as the woman shuffled to the counter, Carol's mental bell rang again. Finally, her brain cells zeroed in on the person from Carol's past Prilla reminded her of—Birdie Atkins.

Decades before, Carol and Birdie had been young teachers in a large, run-down school in Pittsburgh's inner city. Though Prilla and Birdie didn't really resemble each other—Prilla had much lighter hair and eyes—both women had appeared colorless. Neither had much to say. Both bore names that might have been popular with their grandmothers' generation.

As usual, Prilla didn't greet anyone in line. During her weekly visits to Bread on Arrival, she would haltingly answer the questions Carol posed to get her to open up, but she seldom spoke to other customers, a rarity in Loch Mallaig, where everyone knew everyone.

Today, though, the reclusive woman had brought someone with her.

"*Guid mornin'*, Prilla," Carol said cheerfully, her standard morning greeting as inherited from her Scottish grandparents. "We're glad to see you. And who's your friend?"

Prilla gestured toward the newcomer, who was gazing around the bakehouse with wide, wondering eyes. "This is my neighbor, Blanche Geller."

"Welcome to Bread on Arrival, Blanche." Carol held out her hand to the tiny, elderly woman. She appeared even mustier than Prilla, though she wore a cherry-red, knitted scarf around her neck.

Blanche said nothing, but her strong grip surprised Carol.

"What can I get for you, ladies?" Carol asked.

Blanche twitched and muttered under her breath, but Prilla cleared her throat and ordered two of her usual. "Two baps with cinnamon butter, please. And two coffees."

At the mention of the soft, warm roll, an unexpectedly sweet smile crossed Blanche's wrinkled face. It vanished quickly, though.

"So you live in Oppen Woods too?" Carol asked, making conversation as she plated their breakfast. The forested area covered several square miles that reached all the way to Lake Superior. "What a beautiful place, especially this time of year."

Blanche fiddled with her scarf while Prilla handed over money.

"I think the maples are my favorites," Carol continued, "though I'm so glad the pines stay green all winter. Especially at Christmas."

Blanche muttered something Carol couldn't decipher, though she thought she heard the word *faeries*. No trace of a smile.

Of course Prilla didn't smile either, but when Carol complimented her on the Celtic locket she wore, a bit of the dullness in her eyes lifted.

"It's a Celtic Love Knot," Prilla said. "It belonged to my mother. She told lots of Celtic stories when I was a little girl and gave me the locket when I was a teenager." Prilla fingered the intricate silver pendant. For a moment, she appeared as if she might say more, but her face blanked again. "Mom passed away more than ten years ago."

"I'm sorry to hear that," Carol said sincerely. She had been devastated to lose her father, and she knew she would never stop missing him. "You go on ahead to your table. I'll bring your coffee over."

"Thank you." Prilla lifted the plated baps and started toward a table on the far side of the dining area. Blanche trailed after her.

Carol filled two coffee mugs and soon caught up with Blanche, who had stopped at the side window to watch Angus frolic in the yard. His antics inspired Blanche's smile to reappear. "Sweet doggie."

The Scottie had accomplished what pleasantries couldn't: not only a smile, but the first clear words Carol had heard from Blanche.

"Angus loves to meet new friends," Carol said. "Perhaps after you've eaten your bap, you can visit him."

Carol returned to the front counter, but she kept an eye on the two women. While Prilla took her time, Blanche hastened to eat her breakfast, then went outside. Wincing a little as she slowly knelt, the woman pursed her lips as she reached to pet the dog. Angus, sensing a friend, wagged half his body, closing his eyes as Blanche scratched behind his ears.

Prilla's face softened as she watched them. After she finished her bap, she stood up and put her coat on, keeping her focus on the scene outside the window as she did.

"You've got some nerve, showing your face in here," an elderly woman at a nearby table growled at Prilla. "After what you did."

Prilla froze, fingers stalled on her coat buttons.

"That's right," the older lady said nastily. "We all remember."

Carol didn't recognize the other customer, who wasn't a regular at the bakehouse. Although Carol certainly didn't want to alienate their clientele, she couldn't resist the urge to defend poor Prilla. She stepped hastily around the counter and surged forward. "Excuse me, ma'am, but your behavior is uncalled for."

The steel-haired grouch fixed a rheumy eye on Carol. "*Her* behavior is what's uncalled for." She jerked a thumb toward Prilla. "Why don't you ask her what she did twenty-five years ago? Doubt you'd be so quick to serve her once you find out."

With a reproachful grunt, the woman stood and bustled out of the bakery before Carol could respond.

Carol turned to Prilla. "Prilla, are you o—"

"Fine." Prilla fumbled with her buttons, then gave up a moment later. She brushed past Carol, clomping out of the bakery in her sturdy boots. She reappeared in the yard and watched Blanche play fetch with Angus, shoulders slumped and hands in her pockets.

Carol frowned as she returned to the front counter. Her Tuesday regular had made progress today, bringing a friend and opening up a little—until that outspoken customer had ruined everything. *Well, maybe not everything.* If Prilla continued her bakehouse visits, perhaps Carol could figure out just what made the shy artist tick and what might make her feel more comfortable around people.

Carol's heart clenched, as it did every time she thought of her long-ago colleague. She hadn't done much to help poor Birdie. Maybe she could help Prilla. Was her reclusive nature something to do with whatever happened twenty-five years ago? Carol assumed so, and made a mental note to find out more.

Streams of customers came and went. The bakery phone jangled relentlessly, and Carol tabled her concern for the moment. Later, though, during a lull, she probed her mind for possible sources of information about Prilla. Did anyone really know her?

Carol frowned when she realized Hamish was her best bet. Right now, she'd rather not approach him, but Hamish's family had lived in Loch Mallaig for generations. If anyone would know Prilla's background, he would. Hamish enjoyed lecturing from his undeniably vast store of local knowledge. Even more, he loved spouting his opinions.

Carol couldn't help grinning. Though she didn't want to admit it, most of Hamish's judgments proved surprisingly astute.

Right now, he was working outside. Perhaps later today she'd approach him—when Molly was absent—and get him talking. Month of the Faeries or not, that shouldn't be hard.

Carol reminded herself to drink some strong coffee before their encounter—because prompting Hamish to talk rarely posed a problem.

No, the real struggle was always shutting him up.

"This is for me?" Molly eyed the huge basket with mistrustful eyes.

Carol, who had answered the knock at the back door, squinted at the gift basket held by a young delivery man. With its gaudy Halloween cellophane and sparkly orange bow, it seemed very un-Molly-like.

The kid shrugged. "You're Molly Ferris, right?"

"Yes. But who sent it?"

"Nothing on the card." He shuffled his feet, clearly wanting to be anywhere but in the cramped hall with these skeptical women.

Carol gave Molly a little push. "It's yours, okay?"

"Yeah, open it." Laura appeared out of nowhere. "Even if Hamish is behind it, it's not like he'd send you a bomb."

Just a snake—even if it wasn't real. As Molly hesitantly accepted the basket, Carol found herself backing away.

The delivery guy did too. Maybe he'd already delivered too many Month of the Faeries pranks, as he left without waiting for a tip.

Molly seemed to consider following him, then straightened. "This is ridiculous." She carried the basket into the kitchen and placed it on a clean work surface. She set her jaw, untied the bow, and pulled away cellophane that littered her and the floor with glitter to reveal a collection of small, autumn-hued packages of every shape.

Molly stared, dumbfounded. Carol and Laura began to laugh. And laugh.

"Hamish must know you better than we thought." Carol wiped her eyes, then touched a tin of pumpkin spice latte mix and a jar of similarly flavored mayonnaise. "How did he know you can't stand the pumpkin spice craze?"

"I've never told him that." Molly stuck her hands on her hips. "Did you?"

"Would we do that?" Laura fixed an innocent gaze on her friend.

"How else would he know?" Molly grimaced as she searched through the basket, her fingers barely touching each item as though they might bite her. "Pumpkin spice air fresheners. Pumpkin spice salsa and hummus. Pumpkin spice cough drops and—ugh—toothpaste. Gah! Even pumpkin spice kale chips."

Carol shuddered. Though she initially thought Hamish had let Molly off easy, pumpkin-spice kale chips sounded almost as scary as the snake.

Laura nudged Molly out of the way and dug through the basket. "How sweet," she crowed. "Hamish didn't forget Angus. He included pumpkin spice dog treats."

"Ugh! I can't stand the smell." Molly pinched her nose as if trying to keep out any hint of pumpkin spice. "It's bad enough that Hamish dumped all this stuff on me," she said nasally, "but when he pushes it on my dog..."

"You've got to admire the creativity," Carol ventured, then quailed under Molly's glare. "But I promise Hamish didn't get the idea from me. I've never mentioned your pumpkin spice aversion to anyone."

"I haven't either." Laura double-crossed her heart, and Carol couldn't stifle a laugh.

"Some friends you are." Molly surveyed the basket with fresh disgust.

"Seriously," Laura protested. "I don't know how Hamish found out—"

"Found out what?"

Hamish, though not a small person, had perfected the art of materializing out of nowhere, especially this week. Now he aimed a calm but curious gaze at the basket. "Pumpkin spice dog treats? Does Angus like those?"

"*No.*" Molly picked up the package with thumb and forefinger and tossed it into a nearby trash can. "Look, a prank's a prank, but how could you joke about feeding my dog those disgusting things?"

Their handyman quirked an eyebrow. "What prank? I've never seen those treats before. Or this basket." A hint of wickedness gleamed in his eyes. "Though I must say, whoever sent it knew exactly how to get your goat."

He or she certainly did. Carol watched Molly's annoyance give way to confusion. She evidently believed Hamish, who had as good as admitted to his earlier tricks.

Carol believed him too. "Molly, can you think of anyone else in town who knows?"

"Are you kidding? In a town that celebrates the Month of the Faeries?" Molly scoffed. "I've never breathed a word to anyone but you two. Heaven forbid something like this happen." She slapped the basket in irritation.

"Oh, but someone in Loch Mallaig is out to get you." Laura mimicked a monster with fangs.

"No, everybody *loves* me." A tiny twinkle in Molly's eyes betrayed the possibility her irritation was fading.

"Yes they do," Carol asserted. "But what about Grizela?"

Grizela Duff, their town's exacting librarian, had recently given Molly a lecture about an overdue book in front of everyone in Bread on Arrival. Was this her Month of the Faeries version of revenge?

"Maybe." Molly smoothed a furrow from her forehead. "Though I know lots of people who return their books much later than I do. And Grizela is a penny-pincher. Whoever it was spent a lot of money."

"What about Doreen?" Laura suggested. "Though I don't know why she'd pick on you, Doreen's the creative type. She'd come up with an idea like this. Plus, she always knows everything about everyone."

"Maybe." But Molly sounded doubtful.

"Could somebody in your family have sent the basket?" Carol wondered aloud. "Maybe Chloe?"

"No way." Molly shook her head. "My daughter inherited her dad's sensible DNA. Even if she thought up this weird pumpkin spice idea, she wouldn't spend money on something she knew I'd throw away."

Carol probed her memory files for another possibility. "Don't you have a cousin in Houghton who likes to play practical jokes? He lives close."

"You're right." Molly's face reddened again. "Chip knows all about the Month of the Faeries. He is also well aware of my feelings on this silly pumpkin spice trend. It has to be Chip." She pulled out her phone. "I think I'll give my dear cousin a call."

"You might wait till you cool down," Laura said gingerly.

"As if you ever do," Molly countered. Still, she slowly pocketed her phone. "I'll wait until tomorrow, let him stew overnight, wondering if I've nailed him yet."

Laura gathered up the basket's contents. "I need this space," she explained. "I'll put this in the storeroom for now."

"That's as good a place as any until I decide what to do with it," Molly said irritably. "I don't want it in my apartment."

"I'll clear a spot for it," Carol offered.

As Laura hauled the basket into the storeroom, she whispered to Carol, "I hope she doesn't stew too long about this 'gift.'"

Carol shifted a large tub of shortening closer to the wall. "If Chip didn't send the basket, who did? Fergus?"

Fergus MacGregor, Molly's crush from her summer visits to Loch Mallaig as a teen, still lived in town, and he and Molly had rekindled a strong friendship. He was the one who had clued them in to the old funeral home they'd ended up buying and remodeling into their bakehouse.

"But would Molly have told him she hates the pumpkin spice fad?" Carol asked. "Besides, Fergus is such a nice guy—not the type to pull pranks on people."

"Especially someone he *really* likes." Laura wiggled her eyebrows toward the kitchen. "Why would he want to upset Molly?"

They couldn't gab in the storeroom much longer or Molly would come looking for them. As they left, Carol turned her thoughts to the Montrose cakes she had to bake by noon the next day for a clan reunion.

However, as she, Molly, and Laura finished cleaning the kitchen and setting up for the next morning, a clear thought inscribed itself on her mind.

Surely Molly had thought of it as well, and Laura too: whether Fergus, Chip, or someone else had sent Molly the basket of pumpkin spice goodies, Hamish hadn't.

Molly was still on his prank hit list.

3

Hamish was off Friday afternoon, but Carol guessed she'd find him in the town library's extensive genealogy section, a regular haunt of his. He reveled in digging into the past, and no family tree in town escaped his scrutiny. Excited by his research, he'd be in the mood to disperse information.

It would be the perfect time to ask him about Prilla Dunn's background.

However, Carol also knew Hamish hated interruptions, so after greeting Grizela, who confirmed his presence, Carol paged through wedding magazines in the periodicals section for cake inspiration until he appeared at the bottom of the stairs that led to the genealogy section.

Whispering to avoid Grizela's wrath, she asked him, "Did you have a productive afternoon?"

His face brightened. "Aye, discovered a cemetery I didn't know existed. A whole new set of names to explore."

He hadn't bothered to lower his voice, prompting a harsh "*Wheesht*!" from Grizela, who absolved no one from preserving the library's sacred silence, not even friends.

Hamish glared at the formidable librarian, who glared right back.

Carol feared his good mood would pass, so she tugged him out the heavy glass door. "What a beautiful fall day. I'm headed to the loch for a little walk before I return to the bakery."

"Good idea." His clenched eyebrows separated. "Better enjoy the sunshine while we can, eh?"

He seemed to realize she'd forgiven him for the snake scenario, and he offered a joyous recital of gravestone names and possible backgrounds while Carol listened patiently.

As they approached Dumfries Park, she gently steered Hamish toward Prilla Dunn's history. "What do you know about her? She seems so withdrawn, so lonely."

His good cheer waned. "Ah, a sad story indeed. I had Prilla—her full name is Priscilla—in high school. She did her homework, but never raised her hand in class. Never said a word unless she had to. Her half sister, Kristen, was just the opposite. They had a father in common but not much else. Kristen was a year or two younger and only lived here off and on, but she brought along all kinds of strife when she did." Hamish shook his head. "Who would have thought Prilla would be the one to get into serious trouble?"

"What kind of trouble?" Was this what the rude bakehouse customer had been referencing?

He paused. "Twenty-five years or so ago, the lass was accused of murder."

"Prilla?" Carol's pulse skipped a beat. "What happened?"

"She was about to graduate, I think, when she started dating Matt Boersma. An *amadan*, if I ever saw one." He scowled.

Carol recalled many of her former students' names, but Hamish seemed to remember all of his—including the one he'd just called a fool.

"Good-looking boy," Hamish continued, "but all *blether* and no brain." His voice hardened. "Had run through all the girls in his little black book, I imagine, because I remember wondering why he would bother Prilla. She was pretty enough, of course, but she didn't do much to draw attention to herself like the other girls he chased. Anyway, Matt apparently paid dearly for his philandering. He was found in the Faerie Copse—that's a grove in Oppen Woods near Lake

Superior—stabbed to death. Someone had drawn a Celtic death symbol on his face with charcoal."

"How horrible." Carol shuddered. The ghastly event seemed so foreign to this lovely little town, particularly on this brisk, sunny day. "And the police thought Prilla did it?" Carol couldn't picture her plunging a knife into someone.

"They did, and for good reason." Hamish's scowl deepened. "Matt had apparently started seeing another girl, maybe more. Teenage jealousy is nothing to trifle with, in my experience."

"To some extent," Carol said, recalling stories from her own experience with angst-ridden teens but unconvinced it had led to Matt's murder.

"Also," Hamish went on, "Prilla was taking a drawing class in the art department that semester, and they had been doing a unit working with pastels and charcoal. Her charcoal was missing. I don't recall their other evidence, but she was arrested shortly after her eighteenth birthday."

For a moment, Carol couldn't say a word. "Did Prilla just get out of jail?"

Hamish shook his head. "She only went to jail for a few months, though that was too long considering she didn't kill Matt. Turns out she had an alibi."

Whew. Carol was relieved, but at the same time she wanted to blister Hamish with reproaches for omitting that important detail. Instead, she took a deep breath. "What alibi? And if she had one, why did she remain in jail so long?"

"Prilla had her reasons. At the time of the murder, she'd sneaked out of town—didn't want to tell her mother—to see her father. Can't remember his name right off, but he was an amadan too." Sadness softened Hamish's sharp eyes. "The police had wanted to question him about a theft or two in town. Prilla didn't tell them her alibi at first because she didn't want to get him in trouble. And she couldn't afford bail, so she was stuck waiting for trial."

"Didn't want to get *him* in trouble?" Carol didn't know the man, but she could have smacked him then and there.

Hamish read her anger. "My sentiments as well, but unfortunately, Prilla let herself be jailed a while before she told the truth. Then the police couldn't find her dad to corroborate her alibi. The town—well, the entire UP—turned against her, thanks to the media coverage. She retreated to her mother's cabin in Oppen Woods, rarely to be seen in town. Unfortunately, I don't think she could afford to move."

Poor Prilla. Carol couldn't imagine her pain. No wonder she was a recluse. "So her father finally came forward?"

Hamish laughed bitterly. "Only in Prilla's dreams. No one's seen him to this day. Two witnesses who'd watched the story on the news reported seeing her and her father together the night Matt was killed. They were in Isle Royale National Park—you know, right next to the Canadian border—where he probably was hiding out." He shook his head. "If those backpackers hadn't come forward, she'd still be in jail."

Prilla wouldn't stop by Bread on Arrival until the following Tuesday, so Carol spent the rest of her afternoon concentrated on finishing the fondant on a four-tiered wedding cake while Molly and Laura whipped through after-hours cleanup. When all was done, they'd work on details for the bakehouse's upcoming Harvest Party.

Molly had scheduled the event for a Sunday in the middle of October. "Great PR and a chance to show off our goodies," she'd announced to the partners.

And now, Carol noted silently, *a great way to distract you from Hamish's pending prank.*

He'd acted perfectly normal for several days. Though Molly had calmed considerably, absorbed in planning and publicity for the party, she occasionally joked uneasily about what he had in store.

Maybe Fergus could make her forget about it. When he'd heard about their fall bash, he had eagerly volunteered his services and told them he'd show up this evening to help with the planning.

Carol hid a grin as she glanced at Molly, who was examining her to-do list. Did her friend really believe Fergus was motivated only out of the goodness of his heart? Carol had to admit that might be part of it since Fergus had always been community-minded, but she certainly hadn't missed how Fergus nabbed every possible opportunity to be around Molly, even if her friend seemed to be oblivious.

Before long, Fergus poked his head inside the kitchen door and flashed his irresistible smile. "Anybody hungry?" He stepped all the way inside, revealing two large pizza boxes in his hands. The savory aroma of sautéed garlic filled the room.

"I said you didn't have to bring anything." Molly's words reproved him, but she was smiling.

Carol knew her friend's mouth was watering. He'd probably brought her favorite pizza from King's Heid Pub, the four-star restaurant at his resort: deep-dish Florentine.

"Well, if you don't want any, I volunteer to eat your share." Grinning, he slid the boxes onto a prep table. "Can I help you finish anything before we eat?"

"Perfect timing," Carol told him. "After I box this cake, I need a little help taking it to the fridge."

Fergus whistled. "Beautiful job. Some couple is going to be very happy."

"I hope so." Carol opened the big baker's box, slid a spatula under the bottom layer, and slowly moved the cake into the box. Sealing it with tape to keep out the walk-in refrigerator's moisture, she gestured with her head. "Okay, Fergus, grab that side, and we'll put this on the bottom shelf, right side."

Laura held the door open as Carol and Fergus edged the box into place.

Carol wiped away moisture that had gathered on her forehead. She liked baking wedding cakes more than any other kind, but they required endless patience and attention to detail. Early tomorrow, she'd take the chilled cake to the reception site and decorate it with more icing, fresh peach-colored roses, and additional greenery.

Settling at a table toward the back of the dining area, where passersby wouldn't see them and think the bakehouse was still open, they devoured the pizza. Molly consoled a deprived Angus with a dog biscuit, which restored the pep in his step.

Revived and inspired, the group spouted so many ideas that Molly had to remind them the Harvest Party would last only one night. It also should cost less than a million dollars.

Carol, who had headed up many a school fair when her daughter had been young, shared from her extensive store of inexpensive, family-friendly games like donut-eating contests, pumpkin piñatas, and marshmallow fights. She also noted that Jenny, who taught chemistry at the high school, could probably secure them use of the dunk tank the school brought out for their own fairs. Fergus heroically volunteered himself—and his son, Neil—not only to help with any heavy lifting, but to be dunk tank victims despite the threat of chilly weather.

"Sounds like we have that aspect of the party covered." Molly's fingers flew over her laptop keyboard. "Now, before we talk food, there's one more PR stunt I have in mind to advertise the party. I just need to track down some orange hot-air lanterns."

"My sister-in-law made some for Adina's sixteenth birthday party," Laura said. "They were even biodegradable. I'll ask her how she did it."

"Perfect, thanks." Molly made a note on the computer. "And I'll check with the fire brigade about whether or not we can send them up downtown a few days before the party." She grinned at Fergus, a member of the Loch Mallaig Volunteer Fire Company. "Think it'll be okay?"

"I think so," Fergus said. "But you ought to check with the police too."

"Will do," Molly agreed.

"Now," Fergus said, "when the entire UP shows up for this party, what are you going to feed them? A bunch of pumpkin spice stuff, right?"

Molly's grin dropped into a frown so fast it could have caused whiplash.

Carol tried to smother laughter swelling inside, but it burst out as if from a popped balloon. As Laura joined her, Molly glared at them, then looked back at Fergus.

Eyes wide, he spread his hands. "Did I say something wrong?"

"Ignore them." Molly returned her attention to her laptop. "I suppose we'll have to feature a few pumpkin spice scones and cookies, but let's diversify, okay?"

Soon they had added bite-size caramel tarts, apple hand pies, and mini cinnamon rolls to their food list.

As they continued planning, Carol mulled over the flicker of mischief she'd detected earlier in Fergus's innocent face. Or had she imagined it? He'd seemed bewildered at Molly's pumpkin spice mood change, but was it to be believed?

Carol told herself that if Fergus wanted Molly to know he'd sent the basket, he'd tell her in his own time. If and when Fergus did admit his guilt to Molly, though, the fireworks would keep life at the bakehouse—and for all Loch Mallaig—interesting for quite a while.

———————————— ❈ ————————————

Now that Carol knew Prilla's background, she hoped to take more steps in bonding with the forlorn woman. But Prilla didn't show up at the bakehouse on Tuesday to buy her bap, and she didn't come on Wednesday either.

Harvey had always claimed that Carol lost her objectivity when dealing with someone who was troubled or in need, regardless of whether it was a student or an adult. Maybe she was worrying about Prilla for no real reason.

But her mind had hung two sisterlike portraits of Prilla and Birdie on its wall.

Birdie, who had loved math equations as if they were friends. Birdie, who had been eaten alive by unruly students and an unsupportive school administration, then gotten caught up in an even less healthy romantic relationship.

Carol's gut knotted, and she shook away her memories, then redoubled her determination to befriend Prilla.

When Carol asked Hamish if he knew Prilla's address, he'd given it, but advised her not to be too forceful. "Folks who stay to themselves usually have good reasons for doing so. Prilla might not welcome your checking up on her."

Carol didn't like his advice, but she had to admit Hamish might be right. So she fretted about how to proceed until Prilla's familiar dowdy figure finally darkened their doorstep on Thursday.

When Carol greeted her, however, she didn't answer. Prilla's eyes remained as blank as if Carol were part of the wall. She didn't sit before the crackling fire to eat her bap, but hurried to her old truck, which she'd parked out front.

Something was definitely wrong. Had she been scared off by that rude customer the week before?

No matter what Hamish said, Carol couldn't let Prilla simply leave without a word.

Molly was out on an errand, so Carol dashed into the kitchen, where Laura had just finished assembling a pan of Empire biscuits in the kitchen. "Can you handle things alone for an hour or so?" she asked Laura.

"No problem." Laura lifted the tray. "I'll just stay out there after I put these in the case."

"You're the best," Carol said, then grabbed her purse and hurried outside just in time to see Prilla's rusted-out Ford pickup pull away from the curb. Carol trotted to the rear lot and jumped into her own Chrysler 300, then took off in the same direction Prilla had driven.

Carol glimpsed the dilapidated truck a couple of blocks ahead. As she tried to catch up, she wondered about its original color. Maroon, maybe? She'd almost caught up when a blue SUV edged between them. Prilla turned left at the next stoplight, her tires screeching ever so slightly. The light turned red, so Carol took a detour onto a side street in an attempt to parallel the route Prilla might take. When she emerged onto the main road, however, the outdated Ford had disappeared.

Carol searched several streets until she finally gave up. Returning to the bakehouse, she recalled Prilla's haste at the stoplight. Was Hamish right? Was she intentionally avoiding Carol? She shook her head. She likely didn't even know what kind of car Carol drove—and probably wouldn't imagine Carol would chase her down.

"Everything okay?" Laura asked as Carol entered the front of the bakery.

Carol filled in the details about her mission, including Prilla's screeching tires.

Laura patted Carol's shoulder. "Maybe you'll catch her the next time she comes."

Carol appreciated her friend's optimism, but she didn't quite buy it. If Prilla had deliberately evaded Carol, would there even be a next time?

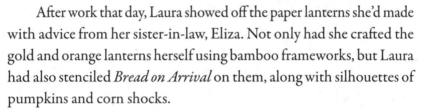

After work that day, Laura showed off the paper lanterns she'd made with advice from her sister-in-law, Eliza. Not only had she crafted the gold and orange lanterns herself using bamboo frameworks, but Laura had also stenciled *Bread on Arrival* on them, along with silhouettes of pumpkins and corn shocks.

"They're beautiful," Carol gushed, thoroughly impressed. "I can just picture these floating in the twilight."

"They are gorgeous," Molly agreed, then bit her lip.

"Before you ask, of course I tested them," Laura reassured her friends. "They'd fly all the way to Oz if we needed them to." She beamed at her handiwork. "Even Brody was impressed when I video called them to show them."

Carol and Molly grinned at each other. Laura was close as could be with her brother, Brody, who worked as a wills and trusts attorney in Marquette.

The next evening, they piled the lanterns and themselves into Bread on Arrival's delivery vehicle—their former funeral home's 1939 LaSalle hearse—and headed for the center of town.

Enticed by a social media post from Molly, a crowd of curious townspeople had gathered in the parking lot of The Hamper, Loch

Mallaig's grocery store. Smiles lit their faces at the sight of the hearse, which Molly had decorated with spooky cobwebs and fake spiders.

After they parked, Molly went to greet the crowd while Carol and Laura set out the lanterns. Laura readied a small blowtorch to light the first lantern, then gave Molly a nod.

"We hope you all enjoy the show this evening," Molly told the crowd, "and that you'll join us on Sunday evening for Bread on Arrival's Harvest Party!"

Once lit, the first bag slowly swelled, *Bread on Arrival* and corn shocks silhouetted against the orange glow. The lantern tugged free from Laura's hand and lifted into the night as everyone oohed and aahed.

Laura sent up the rest in rapid succession. The sky above the grocery store filled with luminous magic.

A movement to Carol's right caught her attention. She loosened her gaze from the floating lights to see Prilla exiting the store carrying bags of groceries.

Prilla stared back, longing in her expression. But the eye contact lasted only a second or two before she whipped around and hurried in the opposite direction, toward a dark side street.

"Prilla!" Carol dashed after her, surprised the woman could move that fast so loaded down. She stumbled as her feet found the edge of the sidewalk.

Carol called to Prilla again, but she detected no movement. She searched a few side streets, lighting the darkness with her phone's flashlight, but saw no one.

How could Prilla have vanished so quickly? And why?

4

"Hold still, Maisie," Carol gently chided her granddaughter as she painted her cheek. "We don't want your jack-o'-lantern to be lop-sided, do we?"

The seven-year-old grinned, her gap-toothed smile so like that of the face painting that Carol had to stifle a laugh. Nothing like grandchildren—and a bustling Harvest Party—to take her mind off Prilla Dunn.

After putting the finishing touches on her masterpiece, Carol handed Maisie a mirror. The child made faces, apparently trying to match the pumpkin's. Soon, though, she remembered her manners and said in a singsong voice, "Thank you, Grandma."

"You're very welcome, sweetie." Carol dropped a kiss on the little girl's head, then Maisie scampered off to find her parents.

Unlike Molly, Maisie's twin, Gavin, loved pumpkin spice everything and had just finished raiding the Harvest Party cookie trays. He'd already decorated himself with orange and black icing that Carol had to scrub off before she could paint his cheek.

"Ow! I didn't want washed." He wrinkled his nose. "I want a ghost on my cheek. Please."

"Okay." She gave his cheek one last swipe and picked up her brush. "One friendly ghost, coming up."

He frowned. "I don't want a friendly ghost. I want a *mean* one."

"I'll give him scary eyes and fangs."

"Awesome." He mirrored Maisie's grin. "I love you, Grandma."

Harvey chuckled from the neighboring booth, where visitors aimed darts at pumpkin-shaped balloons to win a prize. Now that they lived in Loch Mallaig, close to Jenny and Craig, he and Carol had often wondered why they'd stayed in Pennsylvania so long.

Once his face was painted, Gavin sprinted away to show it off to Jenny, who was collecting money at the dunk tank. Tall like Carol, Jenny leaned down to inspect the artwork. She grinned and high-fived her son, then flashed Carol a thumbs-up. Carol smiled and waved back, then welcomed a rare break as her line of little patrons had shrunk to zero.

Harvey slipped to her booth and hugged her. "Nice to see you smile."

When she'd fretted about Prilla, he'd worried about her. Now she returned the hug. "It's hard not to."

The Harvest Party, held outdoors in the bakehouse parking lot, had proved more than successful. The entire town and even attendees from surrounding areas were enjoying the fun games, delicious refreshments, and festive decorations. Laura had set up faux witches gathered around a cauldron filled with dry ice on the front lawn, Harvey had wrapped orange and purple strand lights around the trees, and Hamish had lined the walkway with cutwork paper-bag lanterns—muttering something under his breath about it being better than bread crumbs as he went about the task.

"Everyone is having a wonderful time." Harvey pointed toward the dunk tank and grinned. "Even Fergus. I think."

Carol followed his finger to the popular attraction, lit by more strings of orange lights. As a fundraiser for the local food pantry, partygoers paid a dollar for the chance to throw three baseballs at the lever that would drop Fergus into a waiting pool of water. The water had started out warm but, with the sun going down, had likely cooled by now.

Fergus was teasing his laughing audience. "Ah, you can't hit the target!" he called. "I'm going to stay dry all evening."

Dripping hair and his somewhat bluish skin belied the claim.

Carol shook her head. Fergus had waved off the idea of wearing a wet suit. Fortunately, the evening was unusually mild for October, but she wondered if he'd make it until nine, when the party was to end.

"He's a good sport," Harvey said.

That he was, and as Carol caught sight of Molly making her way toward the dunk tank with a tote over her shoulder, she hoped her friend appreciated Fergus. How many guys would freeze to the bone just to help a friend—even a special one?

Wait a minute.

Carol squinted, trying to see clearly through the people milling under the lights and hanging lanterns.

Molly was handing money over to Jenny and collecting three baseballs?

"Hey Fergus!" Molly shouted, loud enough for everyone to hear. "You don't look wet enough to me."

"I'd like to see you do something about that," Fergus retorted.

Carol blinked as Molly brandished a baseball and began an elaborate windup, to the great amusement of the crowd.

"She isn't . . ." Carol murmured. "She won't."

But Molly did. Though her throw wasn't strong, she nailed the target. With a yell, Fergus plunged into the cold water.

Harvey exploded in a belly laugh, but the teacher in Carol took over.

She strode through the onlookers to her partner. "Molly Kirkpatrick Ferris, what do you think you're doing?"

Rarely had Carol seen that devilish smile on her friend's face.

"I'm simply going to find out the truth." Molly grabbed another baseball. "So stand clear."

Carol stared. "What truth?"

"Yeah, what truth?" Fergus sputtered as he climbed back onto his seat.

"You're going to confess that you went beyond playing a little Month of the Faeries prank," Molly said hotly. "You sent that horrendous basket."

Fergus's eyes gleamed through his streaming hair, but he flung back, "I don't know what you're talking about."

"Yes you do." Molly fingered the baseball. "Say it. Say, 'I sent you pumpkin spice hummus. And toothpaste.'"

A chorus of snickers greeted her accusation.

"Never!" Fergus shouted.

Even without the windup, she sent the ball zinging straight to the target.

Fergus plummeted into the chilly water again with a giant splash. The growing crowd roared with laughter.

"Are you going to keep dunking him all night?" Carol asked.

"As long as it takes," Molly told Carol, then returned her attention to dripping, spitting Fergus. "You sent my darling dog pumpkin spice treats. *Pumpkin spice.* Do you admit it?"

"No way!"

Molly wound up again, and Carol suddenly remembered her playing coed league softball in college.

Plunk. Splash.

As Molly paid for more baseballs, Jenny nudged Carol with her shoulder and murmured, "If Fergus wanted to end this, he could. It's more donations, and I think they're actually kind of flirting."

Of course, her daughter was right. Fergus didn't need a referee to defend him. Carol let a smile rise to her lips.

After a couple more dunks, the gasping resort owner finally fessed up. "All right, all right. I sent that basket."

Molly put her hands on her hips in triumph. "So, the truth finally comes out. And how did you find out that I *hate* pumpkin spice stuff?"

"Can I help it if your cousin Chip likes to play golf at Castleglen?"

Frowning, but with a twinkle in her eye, she tossed her last baseball up and caught it playfully. "You'll never do it again, right?"

"Promise." He held up dripping hands in surrender. "Just *stop*, for heaven's sake."

He climbed out of the tank. Carol and Jenny joined in the loud applause from the audience. Sympathetic bystanders handed shivering Fergus a blanket.

However, Molly wasn't finished. "I have a present for you, Fergus."

In the face of her wicked smile, several around him took a step back.

Fergus, however, lifted his chin and accepted the big, beautifully wrapped package Molly had pulled from her tote. "Do I open it now?"

"It will help you warm up," she said coyly.

"I'm all for that." He slid the ribbon aside, tore off the paper, and opened the box to reveal a bright green Michigan State University sweatshirt and hat.

A new shout of laughter arose from the crowd. Jenny groaned, and Carol giggled until she had to hold her aching sides.

Fergus, who had gone to Northwestern University and had grown up a dyed-in-the-wool University of Michigan fan, hated all things Michigan State. He clutched his heart. "How could you?"

"Now you understand how I felt about a pumpkin spice basket." Molly extended her hand. "Are we even?"

"Even?" Carol rolled her eyes. "She half-drowned him."

"But he got her attention," Jenny said softly. "Not that I approve of these Month of the Faerie shenanigans, mind you. My students make my life miserable for weeks."

"Apparently misery loves company," Carol murmured back as she watched Fergus put an arm around Molly's shoulders.

"You are all witnesses," Fergus announced. "We are officially even."

Amid the townspeople's cheers, he didn't release her right away. Carol didn't miss that he squeezed Molly's shoulders, then smiled down at her when she glanced at him. She beamed back.

Jenny grinned. "Maybe pranks aren't so bad after all."

"Maybe," Carol agreed. "I feel like flowers and a box of chocolates would have been a lot easier, but to each their own, I guess."

Prilla didn't come to Bread on Arrival Tuesday for her usual bap and cinnamon butter. As Carol locked the bakehouse door that afternoon with a resolute click, she decided she didn't want to wait another week to see if Prilla would show up again.

While she and her partners finished cleaning the kitchen, she told them, "Hamish gave me directions to Prilla's house, so I'm going to pay her a visit this evening."

"She lives in Oppen Woods doesn't she?" Molly asked, then frowned at the dark clouds in the sky that were getting no help from fall's rapidly shortening days. "It's already near sundown. I hope you're taking Harvey with you."

"He's interviewing someone for a freelance article tonight," Carol answered. "Besides, he thinks I'm being a worrywart."

"If you go by yourself, *he's* the one who will worry—with good reason." Laura was as cautious about hazards waiting in the forest as she had been about dangers lurking down dark NYC alleys. "I'm going with you."

Carol tried to refuse Laura's offer, thinking Prilla might open up better if she went alone. Still, she couldn't deny the relief that sprang up when her friend insisted on accompanying her.

A short while later, as she turned onto yet another gloomy gravel road that led deeper into a section of Oppen Woods she'd never been to, Carol gave thanks for Laura's presence. Finally, they pulled up and climbed out in front of a small, solitary house surrounded by bramble. There was no sign of Prilla's truck in the rutted dirt driveway, but perhaps there was a garage around back that they couldn't see in the scant forest lighting.

"If I lived alone out here," Laura said, "I'd light up my yard like a stadium."

"I imagine she's on a tight budget, with no extra money for light displays." Was Prilla home? Carol did detect a dim glow in one part of the house. She flicked on her phone's flashlight and aimed it toward the front door.

"Keep that light down," Laura whispered. "I'll bet a gazillion snakes live around here."

Thanks, Laura. But Carol's concern for Prilla kept her from running back to the car.

As they slowly made their way along a path full of bumpy pine roots, Carol realized the rustic house was a hand-hewn log cabin, obviously built more than a century earlier. How long had Prilla's family lived here? Had it been handed down for generations?

Carol thumped on the stout wooden door. No answer.

"There's a light on inside," Laura whispered.

"I know." Carol's heart sank. "Maybe Prilla doesn't answer her door after dark."

Laura folded her arms over her chest. "I wouldn't if I were her."

On impulse, Carol turned the doorknob. After momentarily giving a rusty resistance, the door creaked open. She caught her breath, then called softly, "Prilla? It's Carol and Laura from Bread on Arrival."

Silence. Carol called louder, but nothing besides the hoot of an owl answered.

"This is like a creepy movie," Laura said. "Should we call the police?"

"Maybe she leaves the door unlocked all the time," Carol said, but she didn't believe it.

"Don't go in there," Laura warned. "She'll charge you with trespassing."

But Carol felt her resolve hardening. "Prilla may need help. Do what you want, but I'm going in whether she charges me or not. I couldn't live with myself knowing I could have helped her when she needed someone most, but didn't."

Laura glared at her. "When you put it that way, I guess we don't have a choice, do we?"

They stepped inside the cabin, Carol casting her flashlight beam around what appeared to be the main room. A sagging sofa and a rocking chair that listed a bit to the side huddled near a stone fireplace filled with half-burned logs and dying embers. Dim light shone from a naked bulb above a rough wooden table near an old range, refrigerator, and sink on the other side of the room.

Carol took a few steps closer to the kitchen area, where unwashed plates and lipstick-stained foam cups were scattered about. Half-eaten bags of chips, pizza boxes, and other trash littered every surface.

"What a mess." Laura wrinkled her nose.

"At the bakery, Prilla always cleans up after she eats her bap—even scrapes her crumbs off the table." Carol shook her head. "She may wear outdated clothes, but she's always clean and neat."

"Could we be in the wrong place?"

"No, this is the location Hamish described." Carol gestured to a small counter cluttered with wood scraps and tools. "And I bet that's where Prilla creates her art."

"I guess." Laura sounded unconvinced.

Carol headed for a rustic ladder attached to the wall.

"You're climbing that thing?" Laura crossed her arms. "Looks like a broken neck waiting to happen. And how do you know that floor up there will hold you?"

"The ladder seems sturdy enough." Carol tried to make climbing appear easy. "Maybe I'll find something that will tell us what's going on with Prilla."

Reaching the top, Carol shone the flashlight around the dark loft. No Prilla, asleep or otherwise.

A ratty, plaid sleeping bag and flat pillow lay on the floor, along with a backpack made of holographic rainbow vinyl and an entire wardrobe of very un-Prilla-like clothes. Sequins and rhinestones glittered as Carol's flashlight shone on jeans, skimpy tops, and sparkly stilettos.

Maybe we are *in the wrong house.* Carol's throat tightened. Laura might be right about trespassing charges. Perhaps they should leave, and quickly.

But then she saw a cot with its blankets neatly tucked in and small bureau in one corner, where a gingham curtain likely hid hanging clothes.

She picked her way across the room—the floor seemed solid—and slid the curtain aside to reveal two simple cotton dresses, a couple of droopy sweaters, and a long skirt. Carol was almost certain she'd seen Prilla wear one of the dresses. She opened a bureau drawer and saw plain socks folded neatly inside.

She glanced at the log wall above the bed. An intricate picture with two interwoven symbols—Celtic, no doubt—was burned into the wood. The imagery spoke of Prilla so clearly, it made Carol miss her. Where was the reclusive woman now?

"Are you all right?" Laura yelled from below. "What's up there?"
"I'm fine," Carol called back. "I'll come down and tell you after I've checked a few more things."

She examined the bed. Red lipstick stained the pillow. Had Prilla given her bed to her flamboyant visitor?

Carol knew that opening the backpack was stepping even further over the line, but she wanted to check for an ID. Carol unzipped the main compartment, but discovered no clues to the owner's identity, only more glitzy clothes and an extensive makeup collection. At the bottom of the bag, her fingers found a pendant and chain. Carol pulled it out and shone the flashlight on it.

She immediately recognized Prilla's Celtic locket, given to her by her mother. Carol had never seen another one like it.

Despite the loft's chill, her cheeks heated. Had Prilla given it to her visitor? Carol doubted it. More likely, the woman had stolen her hostess's precious memento. Yet Prilla's guest hadn't felt compelled to conceal it in a better hiding place?

Despite confusion, Carol's sense that something was wrong grew into a conviction. One that required calling the police and confessing that she and Laura had entered Prilla's house.

Carol set the locket on the bureau. Why hadn't she thought of preserving fingerprints? She placed the backpack where she found it, then descended the ladder and told Laura about her findings.

Her partner agreed that they should call the police. "Since this was your idea, you can do the honors."

"Thanks, friend." Carol grimaced as she pulled out her phone, but Laura was right. Hopefully Chief Owen Thomson, the conscientious, reasonable police chief who had worked with them before, would prioritize addressing their concern over chastising them for trespassing.

He did listen patiently to Carol's account, noting that he hadn't seen Prilla around town lately either. His voice tightened, however, when Carol told him about the locket. "At this point, assuming it was stolen is going too far," he warned. "However, I agree that we should check this out. I'll send an officer. Please stay there to answer any questions."

"Of course," Carol said meekly, and hung up.

Fortunately, Thomson sent Greer Anderson, who seemed to understand the implications of one woman's treasure found in another's backpack.

Still, as she examined the necklace with her gloved hands, Greer reprimanded Carol about handling the locket. "I doubt we can learn much from it now." She straightened. "But I think you may be right: something's wrong with this whole picture. Though I don't know Prilla well, I've seen her around town all my life. This locket looks exactly like the one she's worn since forever. And she rarely hangs out with anyone—certainly not with a fashionista."

"We can't believe she'd live like this either." Laura waved a hand at the room. "Would Prilla have tolerated this mess?"

"She may not have made a guest clean it up, but I bet Prilla would have done it," Carol declared. "That's what makes me wonder if she was here."

Laura gaped at her. "Are you suggesting that someone might have been staying here while she was gone without her knowledge?"

"That's exactly what I'm suggesting." Another idea occurred to Carol, one she wished she'd thought of earlier. "On the other hand, Hamish once told me he taught both Prilla and her sister in high school, a sister who wasn't anything like Prilla. Maybe she's the one staying here? Perhaps with Prilla's permission while she's out of town?"

"A house-sitting sister is a much nicer, and probably more likely, scenario," Greer said gently.

Carol's face heated with embarrassment. This could all be a misunderstanding, and she had assumed the worst immediately. Prilla could have even given her sister the locket as a gift.

Greer frowned. "But Prilla has always worn that locket. If she was going to give it to her sister, why now?"

The doubt in Greer's tone encouraged Carol. Prilla did say her mother had died years before. The timing seemed random for her to gift it to someone.

As Greer further examined the cabin, Carol recalled the pride and tender remembrance in Prilla's eyes when Carol had complimented the locket. As different as she and this theoretical sister appeared, Carol couldn't imagine they were close enough to warrant such a sacrifice. She said as much to Laura.

"I agree." Laura sniffed. "If I had a sister who trashed my house like this, no way would I give her anything except directions home."

"Besides"—Carol prodded her memory—"I think Hamish mentioned that Prilla had a *half* sister. Same father."

And if they didn't share a mother, Carol realized, the chances of the locket's being stolen increased substantially. Why would the sister want something that had belonged to Prilla's mom?

Laura's stomach gave a sudden growl, to which Carol's stomach replied.

"You think our tummies are trying to tell us something?" Laura gestured toward the door.

Greer must have heard the noises from across the room, because she chuckled. "Feel free to go. If I have any other questions, I'll contact you."

Over steaming mutton pie at Neeps and Tatties, Carol and Laura pondered and puzzled about their evening.

Carol finally said, "After we tell Molly about all this, let's bounce it off Hamish. Maybe he can give us direction. Otherwise, we'll just have to wait to see if the police can find Prilla."

Laura wrinkled her nose. "I know that's what we're supposed to do, but I hate waiting."

"I do too." Carol patted her friend's arm. "Maybe something will develop faster than we think."

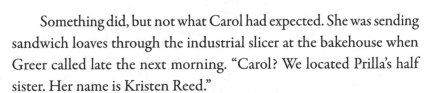

Something did, but not what Carol had expected. She was sending sandwich loaves through the industrial slicer at the bakehouse when Greer called late the next morning. "Carol? We located Prilla's half sister. Her name is Kristen Reed."

"Is she house-sitting for Prilla?" Carol asked, eager for the officer to confirm that Kristen had simply been minding the cabin while Prilla was out of town.

"I'm afraid not."

Disappointment tinged with confusion swamped Carol. "Does she know where Prilla is?"

"No." Greer hesitated, then cleared her throat. "We found Kristen stabbed to death in Faerie Copse, with a Celtic death symbol drawn on her face."

5

At the shocking news, all the air went out of Carol's lungs.

Molly, also working in the kitchen, stared as Carol coughed and struggled to reply.

Greer saved her the trouble of coming up with an appropriate response. "Kristen had been dead only a few hours. The K-9 unit found her."

"Have you found Prilla?" Carol choked into her phone.

"No." Greer didn't elaborate.

Carol knew instantly that Prilla's sudden disappearance made her the primary suspect in Kristen Reed's death. The abuse of the cabin, the locket incident—both seemed to confirm her possible motive: long-simmering sibling rivalry that had boiled over.

Carol forced herself to form words. "Where is Faerie Copse? It sounds familiar."

"It's not a town. It's a small grove of birch trees in Oppen Woods, not far from Prilla's cabin." Greer paused. "I suppose I should tell you, because the newspapers will connect the dots anyway. Faerie Copse is where Prilla's ex-boyfriend, Matt Boersma, was found stabbed to death twenty-five years ago. Nearly to the day."

With the same symbol on his face. Carol grasped the edge of a prep table to steady herself. "But Prilla had an alibi for Matt's murder," Carol protested weakly. "At least that's what Hamish told me."

"As usual, Hamish was right," Greer agreed. "Maybe Prilla has an alibi in her sister's case too. But we won't know it unless she tells us.

If you see her, will you please ask her to drop by the station? We want to get this cleared up as soon as possible."

"I understand," Carol managed to say, wondering why anyone thought Prilla might listen to her.

"Thanks, Carol." Greer ended the call.

Tears welling, Carol summarized the call for Molly. "But we haven't seen her for days. She doesn't know we care about her. That anyone cares."

"I think she knows you care," Molly assured Carol. "Maybe she'll grow tired of running and confide in you."

Carol tried to absorb her friend's positive words, but her heart sank like a fallen cake. Thoughts of Birdie crept through her mind again.

She'd cared about Birdie too, but the young woman, besieged by students and administration alike, hadn't known that. If she had, her life might have been different. Maybe Birdie wouldn't have quit teaching forever. Maybe she wouldn't have let that creep—Winston, was it?—talk her into a relationship that resembled a prison sentence.

Carol closed her eyes, trying not to picture Prilla in real prison, this time for life.

She wanted to call Harvey, but her foray into Prilla's cabin had already concerned him. What would her husband say when he heard about Kristen Reed's death?

———————————— ✦ ————————————

Harvey didn't say much—a reaction that only increased Carol's angst. When outgoing Harvey clammed up, that signaled trouble on the home front.

The next day, her silent husband sat beside her on the sofa. When he handed her the latest edition of Loch Mallaig's *Crown Press News*, she expected the worst from the newspaper, which had a reputation for embellishing stories.

Carol tried not to groan. One corner of the front page reported the local impact of investment thefts by a Detroit con man, Mark Nilson, alias Marshall Hale. The rest of the page—indeed, most of the paper—screamed news of the murder, especially its salacious ties to Matt Boersma's killing.

Carol stared at giant photos of both Prilla and Kristen. Prilla's image seemed to be her high school senior picture. Although certainly older now, she hadn't changed much. Kristen's photo appeared newer, a glamorous pose that showed off long, black hair and a bewitching smile. Only similarly pale eyes—solemn in Prilla's picture, sparkling crystal in Kristen's—hinted that they were sisters.

"Nothing like great photos to sell a story," Harvey said drily, then he narrowed his eyes. "Wait. I recognize her."

"You do?" Carol examined the photo again. "You're right. She was the woman in Neeps and Tatties who walked out on her bill."

"She certainly left an impression," Harvey muttered.

The paper had also published a picture of Prilla's long-ago boyfriend, in which he appeared to be more a member of a trendy boy band than a high school student. Beside that image was a photo of where his body had been discovered years earlier and a rendering of the Celtic symbol found on his and Kristen's faces.

Skimming the stories, Carol noted that twenty-five years before, the police had found the murder weapon, a knife, buried not far from Faerie Copse. She saw no mention of the weapon used in Kristen's stabbing. While the accounts included known facts about both murders, speculation mushroomed in every paragraph. The reporters didn't directly accuse Prilla. Nevertheless, they emphasized repeatedly that she was the common factor in both killings.

One story reviewed the murders that neighboring towns Copper Harbor and L'Anse had experienced during the past six months. The not-so-subtle article suggested that Prilla, the quintessential recluse, might even be a serial killer.

Carol slapped the newspaper with her hand. "This is awful."

"I agree." Harvey pointed to paragraphs she hadn't noticed. "And here's your name in the middle of it all. Here too."

She inhaled sharply. Yes, she'd called the police out to Prilla's, but why did the writer have to include her name, not to mention the names of her partners? They'd helped solve a few local mysteries, but—

"Not exactly the publicity Bread on Arrival needs." Harvey's lips tightened.

"I know." Carol rubbed knotting muscles in her neck.

"But that's not my biggest concern." Harvey slipped an arm around her. "What if this woman comes after you?"

Carol stared up at him. "Prilla isn't 'after' anyone. She hasn't murdered anyone, and she's certainly not a serial killer."

"How can you be so certain?"

I just know. Instead of saying that out loud, she countered, "First, Prilla had an alibi in Matt Boersma's murder. Remember?"

"Yeah, you told me. Hikers saw her and her dad in Isle Royale National Park."

Carol pointed at the newspaper. "Second, this stuff about Prilla's connection with the Copper Harbor and L'Anse murders is all conjecture. They don't present even one fact to back it up."

"I didn't mean to imply that Prilla Dunn is a serial killer. But I am saying she's a primary suspect in her sister's death." Harvey looked Carol straight in the eye. "Right?"

Carol couldn't deny that Prilla was a *suspect*, but she muttered, "Prilla didn't kill Kristen."

He snorted. "And you know this how?"

"I just *know*." The words sounded even less convincing outside her brain, but Carol continued, "Sure, gut reactions don't always pan out. But you've had to trust yours as a journalist, haven't you? And my intuition has come in handy a few times."

Harvey rolled his eyes, but both knew his instincts had steered him toward award-winning stories. And Carol's immediate distrust of an honest-faced Pittsburgh real estate agent had saved them thousands of dollars.

She flapped the newspaper at him again, pointing to the con man story. "Hey, if these investors had listened to their instincts, maybe this Mark Nilson guy wouldn't have cheated them."

"You're trying to change the subject," Harvey retorted.

"I'm just saying that gut reactions can be valid." She kissed his cheek. "After all, the moment we met, we knew we had something special, right?"

Harvey's frown melted.

"I'm sure Prilla didn't kill anyone," Carol said firmly. "And that she needs a friend."

"Okay, okay." Harvey shook his head, but he hugged her again. "All I'm asking is that you show some restraint in helping this friend. Let the police do their job. Don't try to do it for them."

Carol agreed. Privately, though, she noted that her definition of using restraint might differ from Harvey's.

He read her mind. "If Prilla contacts you, let Chief Thomson know." When Carol hesitated, he pressed the issue. "I just want you to stay safe."

"I've never made *you* promise to stay safe," she reminded him gently, thinking of all the dangerous leads he'd chased as an investigative reporter.

He drummed his fingers on the sofa arm, then smacked it with an air of surrender. "All right. I'll trust you on this. I'll even help you, if that's what you want."

He continued before she had a chance to savor her victory fully. "Because it's the only way I can keep an eye on you."

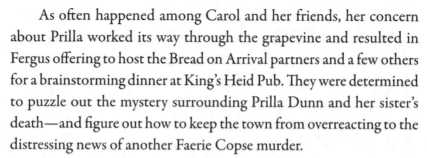

As often happened among Carol and her friends, her concern about Prilla worked its way through the grapevine and resulted in Fergus offering to host the Bread on Arrival partners and a few others for a brainstorming dinner at King's Heid Pub. They were determined to puzzle out the mystery surrounding Prilla Dunn and her sister's death—and figure out how to keep the town from overreacting to the distressing news of another Faerie Copse murder.

The friends chatted about inconsequential things during a decadent dinner, during which Carol mentally pledged more than once to eat salad the next day. "Fergus, I can't thank you enough for this," she said as she placed her fork down after dessert. "The beef and Yorkshire pudding were wonderful. And the tarts were unreal."

Although Bread on Arrival typically provided The King's Heid Pub with their dessert selections, the restaurant's talented chef must have been feeling adventurous that day, as he'd also baked gooseberry tarts with crème fraîche.

"Always great to eat a dessert I didn't make." Laura waved her fork, which held the last bite of her tart. "Especially if it's as delicious as this."

Fergus grinned. "High praise indeed. I'll be sure to pass it along."

Carrying a pitcher of ice water like one of his waiters, the host made his way around the large table in one of the restaurant's private dining rooms. Though he talked and joked readily with Carol, Harvey, Laura, Hamish, and Joyce, he lingered a little longer at Molly's place. After his prank, they seemed to have made peace, thank goodness.

Hopefully this excellent dinner would set the stage for good dialogue about how to help Prilla—and how to help keep their town from succumbing to the near hysteria being encouraged by the *Crown Press News* and a variety of panic-mongering social media reports.

She hated to mess with the fun evening, but after coffee was served, Carol held up the latest edition of the *Crown Press News*. "Has anybody read this yet?"

Molly pulled a face. "Ghoulish."

"Like a terrible horror movie." Laura rolled her eyes. "Why can't they go back to reporting the sanitation board minutes and who won at senior-center bingo?"

Hamish harrumphed. "Trash. It's got everyone up in arms for no good reason."

Joyce calmly patted her husband's hand. "People have let their imaginations get out of control," she said, "but I think that as the police investigate, they'll settle down." Her gentle tone eased the atmosphere a bit.

"Seems to me that the best thing we can do is to help find Prilla Dunn and convince her to turn herself in," Hamish declared.

"You think she's guilty?" Carol's voice was shriller than she would have liked, but she couldn't help herself.

"I dinnae say that." Hamish spread his hands, his agitation thickening his Scottish burr. "I simply said that we should find her. Regardless of her guilt or innocence, people would sleep better at night if we all knew where she was. In addition, Prilla might provide important clues as to who actually committed the murder."

"So you think the odds are good that she's innocent," Carol pressed.

"With no evidence, I cannae say for sure," Hamish replied. "But she should be considered innocent until proven guilty." His voice softened. "Besides, it's hard for me to imagine Prilla harming anyone."

"Same here," Joyce declared. "First of all, it seems totally out of character. Second, Prilla's put up with her sister for years. I don't know either of them well, but I do know that when Kristen hit bottom, she'd show up and mooch off Prilla before disappearing again." Joyce's kind face saddened. "Years ago, Kristen sometimes dropped off her baby, and Prilla would take care of him for days, even weeks. But it's been ages since I've seen the child. He must be about eighteen now."

Kristen had a son caught in this mess too? Carol didn't want to think about it.

"But if Kristen's been taking advantage of Prilla for years, why kill her now? And why make it look like a copycat for Matt's murder?" Fergus mused.

"I don't know about the details, but as for a motive . . ." Laura shifted awkwardly. "There's the locket, you know."

As the other women exchanged glances, Carol stared down at her fingers, which were now entwined with Harvey's. Could that theft have been the last straw for Prilla?

Pushing the thought to the back of her mind, she released Harvey's hand and grabbed the newspaper again. "Kristen's obituary was published today. Her wake is tomorrow, and the funeral will be Sunday afternoon in Marquette. Do you think there's a chance Prilla will show up?"

A series of shrugs were the only response.

"I really have no idea either," Carol went on, "but I've found you can learn a lot at funerals. So I'd like to attend both the wake and the service." She turned to her partners. "That is, if you don't mind covering the bakery. I could make it back by Sunday night."

"You know we're glad to help any way we can," Molly said.

"Speak for yourself, girl," Laura quipped, but she smiled at Carol. "I believe we all agree that we should try to find Prilla. Or at least try to dig up any information that might help solve Kristen's murder."

A murmur of assent went around. Carol saw nothing but support in their faces, including her husband's, though his also carried a note of regret.

Harvey shifted in his chair. "I wish I didn't have that major phone interview tomorrow, but that's the only time my source is available."

"I'll go with Carol," Molly offered, then bit her lip.

"Angus can stay with me," Laura said, picking up on the source of Molly's hesitation.

"He'll love that," Molly replied.

"He's always welcome at the cottage." Laura shot a glare at Hamish. "As long as he stays away from my baking dishes."

Ignoring Laura's dig, Hamish and Joyce said they'd pitch in, not only with serving bakehouse customers, but with the deep cleaning they often did on Saturday afternoons after closing.

Carol thanked them all again and again. Everyone should have such amazing friends. She wondered if Prilla would be grateful for them too, if she knew what they were doing for her.

Before the thought had solidified in her mind, though, Carol revised it when another horrifying possibility hit. What if Kristen hadn't been the killer's only victim? What if she was simply the only one who had been found so far?

Yes, Prilla should be thankful. If she's still alive.

6

Fergus showed up at Bread on Arrival the next morning because, having dreamed about eating a plateful of the bakehouse's apple Danish, he couldn't survive the day without eating at least one. He talked Carol and Molly into drinking coffee with him for a few minutes before they departed for Marquette.

Sitting with them at a table near a window that let in plenty of fall sunshine, Carol grinned inwardly. She suspected Fergus considered her presence optional. Nevertheless, she enjoyed their light moments together before setting off for an event that would be anything but fun.

She and Molly had just reminded each other that they should leave when Fergus's father, Gordon MacGregor, strode through the door. Though nearly eighty, the tall man was fit and appeared ready to hit the golf courses in Arizona, where he and his wife, Sylva, lived during Michigan's cold months.

Despite now being a snowbird, Gordon kept close ties to the community. Usually, his hearty smile nearly outsized him, and he'd make the rounds of most of the customers in the dining area. This morning, however, he answered hellos with a perfunctory wave or two. Gordon's greeting to his old friend Hamish, who had arrived to help at the counter, seemed forced.

Even that uncharacteristic manner, however, paled compared to the abrupt words he leveled at Fergus. "Need to talk to you," he said gruffly. "Neil told me about the Jansen account, and I remember a few details about working with them that you should know."

Fergus's eyebrows rose. "Sure, Dad. But you're not leaving for Arizona for a few days—"

"Some things can't wait. Business before pleasure, you know." Though Gordon possessed a deep, rich voice, his forced laugh sounded tinny. So unlike his usual self.

Carol tried not to stare, but she couldn't help seeing that Gordon had aimed a flaming arrow of a glare past Fergus to Molly. Was he upset about the Michigan State sweatshirt she'd given Fergus? Gordon was a University of Michigan alum, after all.

Clearly too startled to say anything, Molly remained silent. Unsaid words, however, ignited in her eyes: *Excuse me, but what is your problem?*

"Yes, the world would be a much better place if we all minded our own business." Gordon emphasized the last few words.

Hamish left the counter and approached their table. For once, he turned his volume down. "See here, Gordon. If you wish to discuss some difficulty, please take the conversation to a more private place."

Gordon ignored him and shot another glare at Molly. "I hear you're spearheading some sort of effort to find that woman who murdered her sister."

Carol hastened to correct him. "That was my idea, Gordon, not Molly's. Plus, Prilla didn't kill—"

Gordon shifted his dark glower to Carol. "Then I wish you'd leave my son out of it. He works hard enough without trying to do the police's job for them. All of you do. Interference will do more harm than good."

"We're not interfering with the investigation, Dad," Fergus insisted, his tone stretched thin and taut as wire. "We simply want to help Carol's friend—and this community—any way we can. Which is something you taught me."

His son's annoyance seemed to awaken the elderly man's sensibility. "You always were one to help," Gordon said slowly. Suddenly appearing old and tired, he gestured toward the others. "The rest of you may have great motives too, but you're biting off more than you can chew."

Carol agreed to an extent—but how could they stand by and let Prilla be convicted in the court of public opinion?

Gordon shifted his frown to Hamish and nudged his disconcerted friend. "I'm just trying to keep the kids out of trouble, you know." With another tinny laugh, he bade them goodbye and walked out the door.

Carol fixed her eyes on her coffee mug while they sat in silence for a few moments.

Finally, Fergus's chair scraped against the floor as he stood. "Thank you for your patience with my dad," he said, sounding almost as weary as Gordon. "Though I'm positive he didn't know Kristen Reed or Prilla, this whole murder scenario has really upset him. I'm hoping the time in Arizona will settle him down and make life easier for Mom. He tends to obsess over things that have upset him, and it grates on her."

Molly's expression was sympathetic. "A change of scenery will probably do him all kinds of good. In the meantime, we'll pray for Gordon and Sylva—and for you."

Fergus's eyes regained their smile. "Thanks."

"If things with your father grow too complicated, please don't feel like you have to help us anymore," Carol said.

"Let's not jump the gun," Fergus objected. "Dad acted a little odd this morning, but he's fine. Maybe all he needs is a few rounds of golf and euchre night with his Arizona friends." He crossed his arms in mock defiance. "So for now, and maybe forever, you're stuck with me."

"Lucky us," Molly replied brightly. "And at least your dad didn't tear into me for that Michigan State sweatshirt I got you."

"I didn't dare tell him," Fergus said. "That's something he'd *never* get over."

They laughed, then Molly and Carol said goodbye to Fergus and popped their heads into the kitchen to check in with Laura one last time. After receiving last-minute instructions for taking care of Angus, she sent them on their way with her blessing.

As the women drove to Marquette in Carol's Chrysler, they savored the beauty of pines, spruces, and hemlocks dotted with the rich colors of autumn. The blue glory of Keweenaw Bay as they drove along Lake Superior raised their spirits. Turning inland, they found a cozy little log restaurant along the highway that featured fresh apple dumplings topped with rich butter pecan ice cream.

"All part of our research," Carol told Molly as they devoured the decadent treat.

"No complaining here." Molly spooned up another bite. "Going to both a wake and a funeral requires that we fuel up."

As she continued the drive, though, Carol couldn't help but ponder Gordon's outburst. Fergus had helped with previous investigations, and Gordon had never seemed to have a problem with that. Why would the Kristen Reed case cause him such turmoil?

Molly seemed to be ruminating on the same thing. "Gordon's always seemed cordial when we've talked at church or parties. Do you think he's gotten the idea that Fergus and I are a couple? And that I'm bad news?"

Casting a sideways glance at her partner's suddenly pink, troubled face, Carol sidestepped the opportunity to tease her. "I think you're reading far too much into Gordon's flare-up. Obviously, he listened to rumors and thought you were responsible for dumping complications on his son. But he was mad at all of us."

"I guess."

Carol drummed her fingers on the steering wheel. "Maybe Gordon's afraid. Do you think he might have seen or heard something to do with the murder, and it has him stuck in an agitated state?"

Molly gave her a curious look. "What do you think he might have witnessed?"

"Who knows? I seriously doubt Gordon was traipsing around Faerie Copse the night the murder took place. And Fergus said Gordon didn't know either Kristen or Prilla."

"He and his dad are close. I imagine Fergus knows practically every detail of Gordon's life in Loch Mallaig. Wouldn't he know if his dad had gotten mixed up in that somehow?"

"Perhaps." Carol frowned. "But Jenny lives in town too. That doesn't mean she's aware of my every move."

"Like how you're going to Marquette to help investigate a murder?" Molly grinned. "Chloe doesn't know either. Best to keep our daughters in the dark about this, right?"

"As long as we can, anyway." Though Carol grinned too, unease nagged at her. When Jenny had called after reading Carol's name in the paper, she and Harvey had eased their daughter's concern by saying Carol had only reported a missing friend.

Yet, here she was, on the way to Kristen's wake. She didn't owe her daughter a complete report of her life, but this was starting to feel close to actual dishonesty.

Carol steered their discussion back to Gordon. "He could have known Matt twenty-five years ago. Maybe he was a caddy at the resort or something."

"Maybe," Molly agreed. "Either way, I think he knows more than he's telling Fergus. And he's certainly not going to tell us."

They bandied a few more possibilities back and forth, but as they pulled into Marquette, Carol stopped the conjecture. "We could list a few hundred potential reasons why Gordon acted the way he did. For now, I think we'd better focus on the task at hand."

"Or on this gorgeous view." Molly gestured at the town's picturesque harbor and downtown area, where its history as an iron-ore port blended with parks, shops, and condominiums. "Too bad our motel isn't down here."

With only an overnight stay, she and Molly had decided to reserve a room in an economy chain motel. They reached it a few minutes later and checked in. The room was small and simple, but clean and cozy. It would serve their needs nicely. After freshening up and grabbing a sandwich, they headed to a rather dingy funeral parlor for Kristen Reed's wake.

Only half a dozen cars were in the parking lot when they arrived. Granted, the visitation hours had just begun. Surely more mourners would come to honor Kristen, who had been in her early forties when she'd died, according to her obituary.

Before they exited the car, Carol pulled the clipped obituary from her bag and shared information with Molly. "We probably should know a little more about Kristen if we're going to interact with her relatives."

Kristen's address was listed as Benton Heights, Michigan. Survivors included her mother, Lena Reed of Marinette; her son, Kane Reed of Benton Harbor; her half sister, Priscilla Dunn of Loch Mallaig; and her grandmother, Angela Reed, also of Marinette.

Carol frowned. "No mention of Kristen's father."

"If he was one of those absent fathers, her mom probably didn't see the need to list him." Molly jerked a thumb toward the funeral home, which resided in an old brick building with a wide porch that looked like it might buckle under too much weight. "Want to get this show on the road?"

"No time like the present."

They got out of the car and walked toward the rather unwelcoming entrance. In the foyer, Carol and Molly signed the guest book and paused at a bare table with a few scattered photos of Kristen as a sulky child on Santa's lap, as a middle schooler with thick black eyeliner, as a vampy prom goer, all of which conveyed one thing—drama.

Then Molly pointed to a truly beautiful photograph of her with Kane, her newborn son. The camera had captured the joy and wonder of new motherhood. Maybe there was a sweet side to this woman, after all.

The gentleness appeared again in a disorganized clump of snapshots. In one, Kristen was fitting a darling sailor hat on her little son's head. In another Kristen was smiling at Kane being held by—

Carol inhaled sharply.

A young Prilla held the child, beaming at him as if he was hers.

Molly had spotted the picture too. "Look," she said softly. "There are more with Prilla."

There were only five or six photos, in which Kane ranged in age from babyhood to perhaps kindergarten age, but enough to confirm Joyce's memory of Prilla's connection with him.

In every photo, her face glowed in a way Carol had never seen. But Prilla's presence in the pictures soon ran out. With her absence, most of the tenderness also ended.

A hostile element tainted later pictures of Kristen and Kane. In the most recent one, they wore identical expressions. The dark-haired teen boy's blue eyes smoldered with a glower that made Carol's skin go cold.

Once they'd finished viewing the photos, Carol and Molly entered a cavernous, dusty room with startling cranberry and pink carpet. No sign of Prilla—at least not yet.

At the front of the room, an oak podium held a silver urn with a photo of Kristen beside it. An elderly woman with her hair in a bun and a middle-aged lady with heavy makeup sat in the front row of wooden chairs. Throughout the space, handfuls of tattooed mourners wearing a rainbow of hair colors clustered together, chatting mutedly.

Carol initially feared someone would challenge her and Molly's presence, that their cover story of being friends of Kristen from Loch Mallaig wouldn't hold water. They certainly didn't fit the general demographic, but besides the occasional once-over from one of the other guests, they were left alone.

There was no formal receiving line, so Molly and Carol hovered near the back door for a few minutes while other guests trickled in. As they took in the scene, they overheard snippets of Kristen's history. Her friends recalled her kindergarten obsession with wearing paper crowns, declaring she was a princess. They recounted the devastation Kristen had experienced when her father sold her pet poodle. They reminisced about her shoplifting skills as a teen and the way she could charm any guy into buying her dinner.

While Carol and Molly eavesdropped, a quiet, skinny man with a pronounced potbelly protruding from his conservative suit coat caught Carol's attention. He leaned back in his chair with a casual air, but something about him made Carol think he was listening and watching as carefully as she and Molly were. She guessed the man was a reporter, or maybe a plainclothes policeman, mingling for the same reason they had come—to see if Prilla would show up.

The sandwich she'd eaten turned into a rock in her stomach. What if he arrested Prilla at her sister's wake and took her away in handcuffs?

Shaking off the odd feeling, Carol gestured to Molly that they ought to go pay their respects. As they approached the two women in the front row, the elderly woman pierced them with a sharp glance, her pale lips pressed in a frown. Carol guessed she was Kristen's grandmother, Angela, and that the woman next to her was Kristen's mother, Lena.

With some effort, Carol could see a resemblance between Kristen and the once attractive woman now coated with a thick layer of makeup. The scowl on her face did nothing to improve her appearance. As

Carol and Molly ventured closer, they realized that she was talking continuously, keeping up a stream of bitter rhetoric, reproaching Kristen for all the trouble she'd caused.

"I was twenty when I nearly died bringing Kristen into the world." Lena glared at them as if they were responsible. "When her rotten dad ran out on us, I thought, 'At least, I still have my baby girl. She loves me.'" The woman ground her teeth. "But Kristen turned out to be just like him." She listed all their faults in loud, graphic detail—the lies, the thefts, the betrayals. "Her dad's not even here now. He was never where we needed him to be. Never!"

Carol's throat tightened. Would Lena go so far as to accuse Prilla of Kristen's death, trumpeting it at the top of her lungs? She shot a glance at the man she'd noticed observing those around him earlier, and sure enough, he was zeroed in on Lena's words.

As if the angry woman had caught Prilla's name flitting through Carol's mind, Lena said, "The cops think Kristen's goody-two-shoes sister might have done her in, so I can see why she hasn't shown up. But Prilla?" Her snort sounded like a sob. "I don't believe it."

Carol blinked. Prilla had one unlikely ally.

Lena growled. "Prilla wouldn't even know how to kill someone. Besides, Kristen treated her like dirt for years. Why would Prilla kill her now?" She stared at Carol as though she would answer her question, then spat, "What do you want?"

Flustered by the awkward situation, Carol could only stutter, "I–I'm so sorry."

"That's what Kristen always said." Lena mimicked past conversations with her daughter. "'I'm sorry, Mom.' 'I'll make it up to you, Mom.' 'Why don't you believe me, Mom?' If I heard it once, I heard it a million times in a million ways. After a while, I told her, 'Don't tell me you're sorry. It doesn't mean anything when your actions don't change.'"

Angela tried in vain to calm her.

Carol felt Molly's hand tug on her arm, and she knew it was time for them to leave. They edged away, but not before Lena started a new diatribe about Kane's absence.

"You'd think he'd come to her wake, wouldn't you?" Lena bellowed. "Even though he made sure we couldn't get ahold of him, he should have figured out by now that she's dead. No, he doesn't care even a teeny tiny bit. Kane won't come tonight. He won't come tomorrow. He's got his mama's and his grandpa's bad blood. That whole line is just heartless!"

She screeched the last word so loudly that the funeral director, who resembled a movie caricature of an undertaker, swooped in to shush her.

Many other wake attendees exited along with Carol and Molly. Breathing the brisk October night air as a life-giving elixir, Carol made a beeline for her car with Molly right behind her.

They closed the doors and slumped in their seats with twin sighs.

"In a way, I can understand why Kane wouldn't show his face," Molly said as Carol started the engine. "What a family."

Arriving at the motel, they agreed to get some rest and compare notes the next morning. Molly changed, dropped into bed, and fell asleep almost immediately.

Though exhausted, Carol couldn't follow suit. A mental video of Lena's grief-fueled tantrums looped in her head. She also couldn't get Kane out of her mind. Kristen's obituary had listed her home as Benton Heights in southern Michigan, but nearby Benton Harbor was Kane's printed residence. Was he old enough to live independently? Carol knew he was in his late teens, but she didn't recall whether or not he was of age.

Thinking back on the photographs of Kane being smiled at by

his adoring Aunt Prilla, Carol wondered if he kept in touch with her. Would either of them show up at Kristen's funeral tomorrow?

Carol buried her head in her pillow. After Lena's wrathful tirades at tonight's wake, would anyone?

The next morning, over the motel's no-frills continental breakfast, Carol said, "I believe I can think a little more clearly now."

"I could too if I were eating Laura's Danish instead of this cardboard," Molly said wistfully, frowning at her pastry.

"We'd probably gain ten IQ points apiece," Carol agreed. "Unfortunately, maybe ten pounds as well. But let's try to talk our brains into working without the Danish."

Molly set her pastry down with a dull thud. "Mine doesn't want to remember last night. Or think about today."

"Look on the bright side," Carol offered with false brightness. "At least, Hamish can't prank you here."

"His prank might be an improvement," Molly grumbled. "Besides, I've left my home unattended overnight. Heaven knows what I'll be going home to today."

Carol grinned, then brought them back to the task at hand. "We learned a few things last night. For one, Kristen's mother seems to be in the anger stage of grief."

"You can say that again." Molly's frown deepened. "You don't think she could have"—she glanced around at the other diners and lowered her voice—"killed her own daughter, do you?"

Carol cringed, but she knew they couldn't discount the possibility. "She doesn't seem to hold much love for Kristen."

"From the sounds of it, neither does Kane. Do you think he'll show today?"

"If he does, I bet there will be more fireworks. But if he's as vocal as his grandma, we'll learn a lot." Carol tried to soften her stale English muffin with more jelly. "I imagine Chief Thomson's already checked out Kristen's family. Still, there's nothing like getting up close and personal."

"I can think of better places to be. Like a pumpkin spice factory."

Carol gave a chuckle that sounded bitter even in her own ears. Reminding herself that they were there to help Prilla, she summoned all the positivity she had in reserve. "Even if Kane doesn't show, maybe we can glean a few bits of information from the others."

Molly gave up on the pastry and pushed her plate away. "I can hardly wait."

The gloomy day matched their shared mood as they drove to the funeral home. The weather and wondering about Prilla brought equally melancholy memories of Birdie to Carol's mind, namely the few times she'd seen her after Birdie had taken up with that toxic man. The way both Birdie and Prilla had withdrawn from the world, then disappeared.

"Do we have to stay for the graveside service?" Molly asked as they reached the parking lot. She was usually a good sport, but she was clearly reaching her limit.

"No graveside service." Carol winced. "According to Kristen's obituary, they're going to scatter her ashes in front of her favorite bar."

"Lovely." Molly closed her eyes.

"Don't do that." Carol started up the next aisle. "I need help finding a parking spot."

"More cars than yesterday?" Molly's eyebrows shot up.

"Appears to be."

After parking at the end of the next aisle, they made their way toward the funeral home.

A crash of heavy metal music met them at the front door, so loud that Carol and Molly had to communicate with gestures as they looked for seats in the same room that had hosted the wake. They found two empty chairs near the back of the room.

Several bouquets now decorated the podium that held Kristen's urn, a mix of showy arrangements, stark cacti, and pale pink roses and lilies.

Carol leaned forward. Someone had wedged a small, weedy but artistic bouquet between a vase of flame-colored gladiolas and a glittery pot of daisies. Who would send a homemade arrangement like that to Kristen's funeral?

Since Molly couldn't hear much above the racket, Carol motioned for her to come along. Molly's eyebrows went up again, but she walked to the table that held the urn and flowers.

Pretending to look at other arrangements, Carol noticed the simple bouquet's homemade card said *For Kristen*, with no indication of who sent it. She nudged Molly and indicated the flowers and note.

Molly followed her gesture to the ribbon-tied bunch of bittersweet berries, flowering kale, and grasses, with somewhat wilted black-eyed Susans and tiny daisies tucked in, a bouquet that two girls wandering a Michigan meadow could have picked.

Molly's eyes widened, and Carol knew she understood. *Prilla?*

A gray-haired woman wearing a black polyester pantsuit brought in more flowers and began to rearrange the others.

Guessing she was a funeral home employee, Carol pointed to the wildflower bouquet's card. "Do you know who sent that?"

"I'm afraid not. When I came to work this morning—I was the first one here—I found it on the front steps." She raised her chin. "It's not fancy, but I thought if someone cared enough to bring it, I'd make sure their flowers were included in the service."

"That was wonderful of you," Carol said. "Thank you."

The woman gave them a kind smile and returned to her task.

Walking behind Molly to return to their chairs, Carol wanted to shout in triumph—and frustration. If the kind assistant was the earliest employee to arrive, none of them had seen the mourner who had brought the flowers. If Prilla had crept to the front porch before dawn or late the night before, who could have spotted her?

Carol tried to think, but the continual barrage of music blasted any rational thought from her brain cells. She followed Molly to their seats, where she had to content herself with studying the crowd.

The half-filled room of mourners reflected the odd assortment of flowers. The tattoo-covered, rainbow-haired contingent, some flailing in time to the music, still comprised the majority. Was Kristen's son, Kane, among them? Not that Carol could tell. She also saw no sign of Lena yet, so perhaps her grandson might accompany her when she entered.

A surprising number of elderly people—probably Angela's friends and relatives—had shown up and were braving the music. Carol flinched as her head continued to throb with the current song's heavy rhythms.

Out of the corner of her eye, she saw the potbellied man who had attended the wake. He wore a slightly pained expression, as if the music wasn't to his taste either. Was he a policeman or journalist? What other purpose did he have there?

"Have you seen Kane?"

Carol's brain zeroed in on the name, which had been almost yelled by a teen boy sitting in front of them.

"Nah." Near him, a girl with a dagger tattooed on her neck matched his shout. "Haven't seen him since Christmas."

"Think he'll come?"

"Dunno. It's a long way from Benton Harbor. Plus, you know Kane hated his mom. I never could stand her either, even if she was my mom's cousin. I wouldn't be here, except Mom made me."

Who are these people? Why am I here? Carol closed her eyes, fighting the urge to run.

At that moment, Molly touched her hand in solidarity, and Carol was able to breathe again. She smiled at her friend, the friend who had volunteered to accompany her on this awful excursion.

Lena entered the room, hunched a bit but giving off the same defiant vibe as the day before. She was accompanied by Angela, still stoic.

A slim, ponytailed woman in a mandarin-collar tunic stood and hugged Lena. Tears rolled down the angry mother's red face. She clung to the woman, who gently rubbed her back as she guided Lena to the front row.

The slender woman continued to the front of the room. The music faded, and she began to speak in a mellow yet resonant voice that silenced all chatter. "Hello, I'm Pastor Ellie Crandon of Neighborhood Church here in Marquette. Welcome, friends and family, as we remember Kristen Reed and mourn her passing."

Carol admired the way Pastor Ellie commanded the room as she reviewed Kristen's short life, chronicling a few childhood details and casting Kristen in a positive light despite the evidence that her life had been anything but happy. After the anecdotes, she said, "I'd like to read a story Jesus told, one I shared with Kristen last year."

Pastor Ellie opened a paperback Bible and began to read about the wild, selfish adventures of the Prodigal Son. The dismissive body language of the audience made Carol think the pastor was wasting her breath. At the part where the young man hit bottom, however, she could almost feel the crowd slowly lean forward. Carol did too, thinking Kristen must have related to this particular parable. She wondered if the woman had ever made her own decision to return home and ask forgiveness.

Then Pastor Ellie read, "'But while he was still a long way off, his father saw him and was filled with compassion for him; he ran to his son, threw his arms around him and kissed him.'"

Joy, like a small candle, lit Pastor Ellie's face as she looked up from the reading. "That's what our Father is like. When we admit we've blown it, He will welcome us back, no matter what stupid, hurtful things we've done to ourselves and to others."

Carol risked a glance at Kristen's mother, wondering how Lena was taking this Scripture about a forgiving parent. She sat with arms tightly crossed, wearing a scowl, but made no sound. Carol couldn't help but doubt that Kristen would have received any such reception.

"I know all this for a fact," Pastor Ellie continued, "because like the guy in the story, I've done it all too. Even ended up in jail more than once."

A murmur of disbelief rippled throughout the room.

"The third time, I had hit bottom," the pastor continued. "Finally, at that point, I told Jesus that I'd blown it big time." She paused, then told an aside. "When I was a little kid, somebody took me to Bible school, and to get a plastic prize, I memorized that verse you see everywhere all the time, so much that you barely even notice it anymore—you know, John 3:16. Well, in jail, for the first time, I got it. Really got it."

Carol knew the verse by heart herself, but she felt a warm wave of comfort as Pastor Ellie recited it from memory.

"'For God so loved the world that he gave his one and only Son, that whoever believes in him shall not perish but have eternal life. For God did not send his Son into the world to condemn the world, but to save the world through him.'"

Ellie waved her closed Bible. "Jesus doesn't have it in for us. He wants to save us from the mess we've made of our lives, of others' lives." The pastor's voice trembled. "Did Kristen buy it? We don't know. I hope so." She lifted her chin, and the resonance returned. "But we who loved her can make that choice. Why stay at the bottom when God wants the best for us? Why not grab the best deal we can ever hope to get?"

Her words echoed in the silent room.

Pastor Ellie offered a brief closing prayer, then headed for Lena as the funeral director who had been present the day before began dismissing rows of mourners.

The music swelled to painful levels once more. Carol's head pounded again. So much for information gathering. With this noise, how could she hear anything?

Maybe the funeral director disliked it as well, as he practically raced down the aisle to usher guests out of the room. Carol and Molly followed the crowd outside, where the still-drizzling weather seemed a welcome refuge from the music and sadness indoors. Many of the guests stayed on the porch to continue their pre-funeral discussions.

With the rush of chilly, but quieter air, Carol's brain began to function again, and she tried to puzzle out how to track down someone who had seen the bearer of the homemade bouquet. She glanced at the rundown houses nearby, but at the thought of knocking on doors, an invisible band around her head tightened.

"Maybe we should stay a while?" Molly murmured.

Carol wanted to be anywhere else, but she couldn't argue with that logic. "It's probably our only chance for major eavesdropping."

Molly nudged her and tilted her head toward the front door, where Lena and Angela were emerging, accompanied by a solemn Pastor Ellie. Lena leaned heavily on both women as they exited the funeral home. The gray-haired mortuary assistant trailed behind, carrying Kristen's urn.

As if on cue, the drizzle ramped up to full rain.

Pastor Ellie scrutinized Lena's face, concern coloring her expression. "Didn't you say you left the hospital early?"

"Yesterday morning," Lena answered. "Made it to Kristen's wake with an hour to spare." She swayed.

"Here." The pastor grabbed an aged wicker chair. "Sit on the porch a moment or two."

"I'll never go back to that place again," Lena spat. "Those idiots in Green Bay made me worse, not better."

Gasping a little, Lena plopped onto the chair. Pastor Ellie gestured to a seat for Angela, who also looked as if she longed to collapse.

Now the clouds dumped rain as if from a bucket. How would these two women make it home in this weather?

Before the idea had fully formed in her mind, Carol surged forward. "Is there some way we can help?"

Lena and her mother stared blankly at her, but Pastor Ellie smiled. "Thanks for your offer, but a couple from my church are bringing their car around. We'll make sure they get where they're going safe and sound." She cocked her head, a gleam of curiosity in her eyes as she took in Carol and Molly's conservative attire. "How did you two know Kristen?"

"We're just friends from Loch Mallaig," Carol said hastily, "where she stayed from time to time."

Though the pastor's smile never faltered, Carol wondered if those keen eyes had seen right through her feeble fib.

After expressing final, brief sympathy to Lena and her mother, she and Molly raised the hoods on their rain jackets and sprinted through the pouring rain to Carol's car. Flinging open the doors, they jumped inside.

While Molly emptied water from her shoes, Carol took one more look at Lena and Angela before their ride pulled up. For a moment, she wished she could offer more comfort to the white-faced mother and grandmother. After all, Lena had apparently just left the hospital, and that meant—

"If Lena was hospitalized in Green Bay at the time Kristen was murdered, then she couldn't have killed her," Carol said, pushing damp hair back from her face. She shivered, then started the car.

"Thank goodness. Murder is a gruesome enough concept without adding the possibility of it being done by her own mother," Molly said through chattering teeth, rubbing her upper arms.

Carol felt the same way, though she was unsure whether the bone-deep chill she felt was from running through a frigid rain … or from the idea that a woman could kill her own child. She cranked up the heat. "Let's try to dry out before we start phase two of our investigation."

"Phase two?" Molly groaned. "I thought we were going home after the funeral."

"I did too. But this idea occurred to me—"

"You and your ideas," Molly scolded.

"You say that as if you haven't roped Laura and me into plenty of harebrained schemes yourself," Carol teased.

"It's different when they're *my* ideas."

Carol chuckled. "Finding a witness who saw Prilla sneak that bouquet onto the funeral home's porch is vital to our search for her. I know the last thing you want to do in this weather is canvass the neighborhood, but I don't see how much choice we have."

"Knock on doors? Here?" Molly scanned the houses around them dubiously. "Don't you think we've had enough excitement on this trip?"

"It's broad daylight," Carol said. When Molly raised a brow at her, she amended, "Well, kind of. And we'll do it together. Please, Molly?"

Her partner rubbed her temples, and Carol feared she'd refuse to leave the car until they reached Loch Mallaig.

But Molly relented. "If there's any chance we can confirm that Prilla is here in Marquette, we should do it."

"Thank you." Carol squeezed her hand. "Now let's go before we talk ourselves out of it."

The rain had started to slacken, and by the time they reached the shabby house next to the funeral parlor, it had stopped completely. Carol brightened. Perhaps this was a sign that the venture would go better than they thought.

When a hard-looking woman didn't let them explain their mission before slamming the door in their faces, Carol's optimism level dropped.

"I guess we do look like we've been to church," Molly said, glancing down at her nice top and dress pants. "Maybe she thought we were trying to push religion on her."

The next homeowner, a young man in baggy jeans, listened as Carol told him they were looking for a missing friend. But when she asked if he'd seen anyone around the mortuary between the wake and the funeral, his eyes narrowed to slits. "Are you cops?"

"No, just friends who want to help," Carol told him, then explained about the bouquet.

"Why didn't she just show up at the funeral? Is she hiding from the cops?" The guy's dark brows lowered over suspicious eyes. "I heard that the woman who died was murdered. Is that right?"

Carol's heart sank as she admitted, "Yes. That's true."

"I don't want anything to do with murder." He shut the door with a bang.

After a similar experience with a vague but hostile young woman who lived across the street from the funeral home, Carol wanted to give up, and so did Molly.

"The apple dumplings are calling our names," Molly urged.

"One more?" Carol asked.

Molly must have seen the pleading in her eyes. "Okay." She

glanced at the gray sky overhead. "But it looks like it's going to start raining again."

The posts on the next house's porch needed painting as badly as its neighboring buildings, and rusty patio chairs with torn cushions didn't help the ambiance. But the grass had been mowed, and Carol didn't see a single piece of trash in the yard. A pot of yellow chrysanthemums, like misplaced sunshine, bloomed by the faded door.

When a heavy, pale-faced woman eventually answered their knock, Carol wished she'd listened to Molly. The woman wore an oxygen tube in her nose, and it appeared as though a trip to the door was too much for her. Missing, however, was the knee-jerk distrust that had characterized her neighbors. When Carol introduced herself and Molly and told her they were looking for a missing friend, she wanted to hear their story.

Worn-down outdoor chairs or not, Carol was glad for the invitation to sit.

The woman wrapped a thick sweater around herself, tugged a small oxygen tank outside, and settled herself into a chair. "So you think your friend might have come here? By the way, I'm Mary."

"Thanks for your hospitality, Mary." Carol explained about Prilla and the bouquet.

Instead of staring at them as if they'd lost their minds, the woman nodded in understanding. "So you believe your friend is innocent of murdering her sister, but wanted to leave a tribute at her funeral even though she couldn't attend because she's on the run. You're trying to help her, but she doesn't know that."

"Exactly." *Whew.* Carol caught Molly's relieved glance as well. This woman was treating them as if they were sane.

Mary clucked her tongue. "As far as seeing your friend over there during the wee hours, I'm afraid I won't do you any good. I sleep all night, and usually all morning. Sleeping's about the only thing I do well these days."

Carol couldn't help wilting.

"But I know someone who might have seen her." Mary pulled a flip phone from her pocket, tapped a few buttons on it, and stuck it to her ear. "Hey, Lem. I have some ladies here on my porch you might be able to help." She gave a quick, accurate summary of Carol's story. "Really? Good. See you in a few."

The rain had started pattering again, but Carol didn't care. "Thank you so much, Mary."

"No problem," she said. "I hope Lem can help you find Prilla."

Mary's burly, gray-haired neighbor was true to his word and appeared a few minutes later. "I live just down the street a few blocks," Lem explained, setting his wet umbrella on the porch.

"He and his wife, Sally, have been good friends of mine since forever," Mary said.

Lem sat in the chair next to her. "Yeah, we look out for each other."

"He keeps up my yard too." Mary smiled at the big man. "Don't know what I'd do without him and Sally."

"If I had a dollar for every loaf of that Russian walnut bread you've made for us the past twenty years, I'd be a rich man," Lem said. "Not that I'd ever take the dollars instead."

Sounds like Loch Mallaig. Though Carol couldn't wait to hear what Lem had to say, seeing their friendship warmed her heart like a cozy quilt.

"But we're going on and on." Mary waved a dismissive hand. "These ladies need to hear about what you saw this morning." She leaned toward Molly and Carol. "He delivers the newspaper in our neighborhood."

"It may seem more suited to a teenage boy than a retired Marine, but it keeps me busy." Lem brushed raindrops from his jacket. "Pat and I—Pat's my partner on the truck—we were just starting our route. Must have been about five, our usual time. I'd just finished dropping Mary's paper when I saw a lady in front of the funeral home's front door. Wondered what in the world she was doing there."

Carol inhaled an anxious breath.

"She was kind of tall." Lem frowned. "Wore a bulky coat. Couldn't see what color hair she had because she wore a scarf over her head. Of course the sun wasn't up. But the streetlight was bright enough that when she turned around, I did see her face for a second or two."

Heartbeat thundering in her ears, Carol pulled out her phone. She showed him a copy of Prilla's newspaper photo. "Was this the woman you saw?"

There was no hesitation when Lem answered. "Yeah. It was her."

8

Prilla was okay! As Carol and Molly chatted with Lem and Mary for a few more minutes, then made their way back to the Chrysler, Carol felt hope bubbling inside her like a fountain. Maybe Prilla's story wouldn't end like Birdie's—with a question mark, a story with an ending Carol didn't know. Over the years, she'd tried to find Birdie through social media, but to no avail.

Carol pushed away melancholy thoughts of Birdie and let herself savor the joy and relief of knowing Prilla was alive and at least relatively well for a few minutes.

Then, as she sat in the driver's seat while Molly texted Laura an update, Carol realized that her next step should be filling in Chief Thomson about her and Molly's escapade. She didn't relish the idea of fessing up, though.

On one hand, Carol didn't want to call the chief and reveal she and Molly had gone to Kristen's funeral without his blessing. On the other, he needed to know Prilla was alive—along with any details they could share that would help solve this murder and ultimately confirm her innocence.

Deciding not to delay the inevitable, Carol dialed the chief, who answered promptly. She explained their trip as succinctly as possible, hoping to escape his rebuke. Though Thomson sounded annoyed about their investigative trip to Marquette, Carol could tell that he was also a little impressed by their bravery in facing Kristen's relatives.

"I imagine you've checked into Kristen's family background," Carol said. "Do you know much about her mother?"

"I've been working with the police in Marquette," the chief said. "By all accounts, they had a poor relationship."

"A poor relationship?" Carol choked. "That's an understatement." Recovering her voice, she described the scenes at the funeral home. "If Lena hadn't been hospitalized in Green Bay, I would think she's a far more viable suspect in Kristen's murder than Prilla." She paused. "Is there any way that could be confirmed?"

"I'll look into it," the chief said, his tone entirely no-nonsense.

Now that she'd suggested a more likely suspect than Prilla, Carol shifted to confirming her friend's presence in Marquette. She told him about her conversation with Lem. "He seemed certain that he saw Prilla at the funeral home. He even identified her from the newspaper photo I showed him," Carol reported. "I have no idea if Prilla's still in Marquette, though. It was early this morning that Lem saw her, and she could be long gone."

"She may be gone," Chief Thomson said. "Or she may still be there. Earlier this afternoon, a tall woman who might have been Prilla stopped at a convenience store on the edge of Marquette."

"Someone saw her again?" Carol gripped the phone tighter. Molly lifted her gaze from her own phone's screen, surprise coloring her face.

"Could have." Chief Thomson described a video recorded by the convenience store's camera. The possible Prilla had been wearing a heavy coat and scarf that covered most of her features. After she used the restroom, she bought a pack of gum. "They had no outside cameras, but the clerk thought she got into a car with a man who'd remained there."

"Prilla was with a man?" Carol shot a shocked look at Molly, whose eyes widened. "Did the clerk catch a glimpse of his face?"

"Not really," the chief said. "The guy wore a hoodie that almost covered his face. Clerk said his head nearly reached the roof of the car, so he's probably tall. Also said he hugged the woman a time or two."

Had Prilla found a new boyfriend who was helping her? Or had her pickup broken down? Had she hitchhiked to Marquette with this guy—good intentioned or otherwise?

Carol shuddered and tried not to let her imagination run away. "Do we know what kind of car the man drove?"

"The guy at the store said he thought it was a green, late-model SUV. Of course he didn't get the license plate number."

"At least we know it definitely wasn't Prilla's old Ford." Carol described it for him. "Nobody reported seeing one like it abandoned on the way to Marquette, did they?"

"No," the chief answered. "At least, not yet. I'm glad to know more about her truck. We've got the year and make, of course, but details like yours can't really be recorded by the DMV."

"I hope it helps."

"I'll tell Marquette's police chief about both the car and the sighting. He and I have been in close contact, and I know he's got his best officers on the case. If she's still there, they'll find her."

That felt like a pretty big "if" to Carol. But if Prilla had fled, where had she gone?

Glancing up at the now-empty funeral home porch, something else Chief Thomson said dinged in Carol's mind. "Since you've been in touch with the local police, do you happen to know if a plainclothes officer came to the funeral? There was a middle-aged man here who didn't seem to fit in with the rest of the crowd."

"I believe the chief was planning to send someone, though I don't know who," Chief Thomson said. "He said Kristen didn't mix with the best crowd, and that maintaining a presence, even if Prilla didn't come, might be a good idea."

Aha. Carol reminded herself to tell Harvey her instincts had triumphed once more.

At the beginning of their call, Chief Thomson had sounded irritated, but he thanked her before they hung up—a better ending than she'd expected. Carol leaned back in her seat and exhaled, trying to summon the energy to drive back to Loch Mallaig.

"Wow," Molly said. "Talk about a twist. Prilla was with a guy?"

"If it actually *was* Prilla at that convenience store." Carol's head was beginning to ache. "If, if, if. I'm starting to hate that word."

"You'd better get used to it." Molly buckled her seat belt. "I have a feeling we're in this for a long haul."

Harvey didn't say much, but the bear hug he wrapped Carol in when she walked through the door told her he was glad she was home. She hugged him back, hoping he understood how much she felt the same way.

Though worn out from the struggles of the last couple of days, she insisted on making hot cider before they curled up together in front of the fireplace so she could share all she had done and learned in the last two days.

Harvey was shaking his head before she finished her account of the funeral. When she related how they discovered Prilla's possible presence in Marquette, however, he sat up straight. "You and Molly were knocking on doors in a bad neighborhood? I thought you were just going to the funeral."

"It wasn't *that* bad of a neighborhood. And it was the middle of the day."

"Crimes are committed at all hours."

Debating with him would be counterproductive, especially since she needed him to be on board with her next idea. "Regardless, I am thankful we found a clue to Prilla's whereabouts." Carol snuggled a little closer. "And especially thankful to be with you."

Harvey raised an eyebrow, knowing she was buttering him up. "You've got something else on your mind, don't you?"

"Well, yes. I can't help wondering if Prilla will go to Benton Harbor to find Kane."

His forehead furrowed. "Why would she go to Benton Harbor? That's a long trip just to see a nephew. Why wouldn't she call instead? And didn't you say she had a real lemon for a pickup?"

"First, I honestly doubt she owns a cell phone. Second, maybe that guy she was with took her." A red flag flared in her mind whenever she thought of the stranger, but Carol pushed on. "Anyway, Prilla might go simply because she misses Kane. The pictures showed that they were close at one time. Maybe they still are close—only she and Kristen weren't anymore, so Kristen wouldn't have had any recent photos of Prilla and Kane. Prilla might have hoped to contact him when he came for the funeral, only to be terribly disappointed. Maybe she's worried about how he's taking his mother's death." Carol swallowed. "Especially if he's seen all the online stories that point to her as a chief suspect."

"Lots of maybes," Harvey said, sounding every bit the skeptical journalist.

"Maybe." She threw him a teasing glance. "But all reasonable possibilities that could lead us to Prilla. The way Lena talked—well, yelled—I'm not even sure Kane knows that his mother's dead."

"Isn't telling him his relatives' responsibility?" Harvey remained unmoved.

"You're right, of course. But this is a teenage boy we're talking about."

"From what you've told me, this kid disliked his mother for very good reasons," Harvey countered. "He may be as much a suspect as anyone else, right?"

Carol looked him in the eye. "If he wanted to kill her, why not do it in Benton Harbor? Why would he travel nine hours to Loch Mallaig? That's possible, but it seems highly unlikely."

"Fair point," he admitted.

"Besides, we're talking about a boy with a terribly dysfunctional family. A boy who's lost his mother."

Harvey said nothing for a minute or two. Finally, he gave up. "Even if you went to Benton Harbor—which, I might add, would also mean a nine-hour drive for you—how would you begin to search for Prilla or Kane?"

"I dug around online and found addresses for both Kristen and Kane. That would be a start."

"I suppose I could do some digging and see if there's anything more recent or relevant."

Carol tried to suppress a smile. She'd made her case. Harvey was on board.

She wound her fingers around his. "I know I just came home, but it's really important that we find Prilla as soon as possible." She packed all the appeal she could muster into her expression. "I think I should leave tomorrow morning, if I can get someone to cover for me again at the bakery."

"What do you mean, 'I should leave,' missy?" He stared into her eyes. "I didn't know you were going to knock on doors in Marquette. But I'm on to you now. You're planning to ask around—probably in the worst neighborhood in town—about a murder victim and her half sister who's suspected of killing her. Not to mention Kristen's son, who, whatever you argue, also might have done it. There's no 'I' about this. Attending a funeral is one thing. But letting you take on this fool's errand without me? Not on your life." He pulled her to him in a fierce hug.

Carol returned Harvey's embrace, but her mind began to race. What would they find in Benton Harbor, if anything? Would they locate Prilla? Would they discover clues that would help exonerate her for Kristen's murder?

Suppressing a shudder, Carol realized that absolving Prilla might bring them face-to-face with a cold-blooded killer.

9

Knowing they were up early, Carol called Molly and Laura first thing the next morning to make sure they could cover the bakery for another few days without her. Both readily agreed, saying that between them, Hamish, and their other part-time helper, Bridget Ross, everything would be fine.

Gratitude for such supportive friends surging through her, Carol next called her Aunt June, also an early bird. She'd been meaning to go see her mother's eighty-five-year-old sister for a while now, and the trip to Benton Harbor took them right through Muskegon, where June resided in an assisted living facility. June was overjoyed at the prospect of Carol and Harvey coming to visit, and they quickly set plans for tea that afternoon.

Harvey made calls too: one arranging a supper date with an old journalism buddy in South Haven, and one to Jenny, letting her know they would be out of town for a few days to visit friends and family.

Having listened in on Harvey's chat with their daughter, Carol raised an eyebrow. "You didn't mention that we might look for Prilla in Benton Harbor."

"You know, I didn't." Harvey slapped his forehead in mock astonishment. "Forgot to say anything about Kane either, or that he might have murdered his mother."

Carol clucked her tongue. "They say that memory starts to fail after age fifty."

He grinned. "And doesn't that come in handy sometimes?"

So their journey to southwestern Michigan began with smiles. With an hour's stop at Aunt June's—she didn't have the energy for a long visit—and supper in South Haven, they wouldn't arrive in Benton Harbor until that night. They switched drivers often, though, and the October beauty kept the trip from becoming too tedious.

Aunt June's delight at seeing them brightened their day considerably—though guilt at using the visit as a cover for their fact-finding trip to Benton Harbor tinged Carol's pleasure.

"She enjoyed it, you enjoyed it. Leave it at that," Harvey advised as he pulled back onto the interstate. "Try not to complicate things more than they already are."

Later, when they met his friend for supper, Carol might have offered her husband similar advice.

Charming South Haven featured a restaurant where they could watch the sun set over Lake Michigan. Harvey and Phil Krannert, a pleasant, balding fellow retiree, shared several stories about their escapades as journalists.

But when Phil learned about their mission, he whistled. "Did you know Benton Harbor's violent crime rate is higher than Detroit's nowadays?"

Now you tell me. Nevertheless, Carol set her jaw. Despite Harvey's grimace, additional complications would not stop them.

When they arrived in Benton Harbor, Carol wanted to track down Kane Reed's address immediately.

"Knock on somebody's door in a strange town *at night*?" Harvey snorted. "I don't think so."

He was right, of course, but Carol was sure she'd lie awake all night, her mind spinning faster and faster. It did eventually shut down, and she slept on the hotel's comfortable bed as if it were her own.

Bright and early the next morning, she poked Harvey awake. "Let's try to find Kane first."

He opened one eye. "What, you expect him to open the door at dawn and thank you for waking him up?" Without waiting for an answer, he rolled over and began to snore again.

Unfortunately, Harvey even made sense when half asleep. Carol lay wide awake for another hour, counting the minutes until she could, in good conscience, poke him again. "We only have today to look for Kane."

"Okay, okay." With a groan, Harvey dragged himself out of bed and headed for the shower.

After breakfast, the car's GPS guided them into what appeared to be Benton Harbor's worst neighborhood, which seemed to hold little more than graffitied buildings, litter, and potholes. When they parked in front of a grimy brick apartment building, Carol checked once, then twice to ensure the doors were locked. Recalling Harvey's refusal to search last night, she waited to hear him say, "I told you so."

Instead, Harvey simply said, "I hope we find this guy right away."

If they didn't, Carol told herself that the odds of finding her Chrysler intact would drop drastically by the minute. "I'm sorry I dragged you into this little adventure."

Harvey grinned ruefully. "You keep life interesting."

That I do. She was doubly thankful for his presence as they passed through an unsecured front door and climbed rickety steps to a reeking third-floor hallway. Had the light bulbs been changed in a decade?

When they found the correct number, the young man who answered their knock glared at Carol and Harvey with tired, red-rimmed eyes. "What do you want?"

Harvey offered a smile. "Sorry to bother you, but we're looking for Kane Reed. Does he live here?"

The boy barked a mirthless laugh. "Sure, he lived here for a few months. But if he ever comes back . . ." The former roommate let loose a too-detailed description of what he'd do to Kane.

"I'm sorry," Carol interrupted, "but we're trying to find Kane to tell him his mother passed away."

Had she expected a semblance of sympathy from this young man? Instead, his thin face hardened and he reached for his jeans pocket. "Are you cops?"

"No." Harvey stepped in front of Carol. "Just friends. We thought Kane should know."

"You ain't any friends of Kane or his mom," the man replied with a sneer, "which is just fine with me. But you ain't my friends either. If you know what's good for you, you'll leave."

"We will," Carol assured him. "But do you have any idea where Kane might have gone?"

"If I knew that, do you think I'd still be out five hundred bucks?" *Bang.* The tenant ended his sentence by slamming his door.

Harvey hurried Carol toward the stairs. "Well, that was fun."

She turned to reply, but her mouth trembled. What could she say?

At a movement behind Harvey, Carol jumped a foot above the floor. Harvey spun around, fists raised.

The dark-haired girl behind him held up her hands. "Hey, chill. I'm not out to hurt anybody. Not old people, anyway."

"I'm not out to hurt anybody either," Harvey said stiffly. He never reacted well to being called old.

"My husband doesn't go around looking for fights," Carol said, "but we just met the guy down the hall. Not very friendly. Is he one of your neighbors?"

"Yeah. Saw the whole thing. Darin can get pretty mean," the girl agreed. "Kane was nicer. We were good friends."

Her large, gray-green eyes, edged with heavy liner, betrayed that Kane might have been more than a friend.

"Have you seen him lately?" Carol asked. "Do you know where he's living?"

The girl's focus shifted past her to Darin's door.

Carol understood her caution. Fresh air would also be nicer than this musty hallway. "Let's go outside."

The young woman followed them to the building's decaying front stoop, where she and Carol sat in the sunshine while Harvey stood off to the side, letting his wife take the lead. The girl stared at her slender hands instead of making eye contact.

"Kane's mother died, and we're not sure he knows," Carol explained. "That's why we want to find him."

The girl twisted a lock of her long, purple-tinged hair. "When did she die?"

"Just last week."

"Maybe his aunt already told him."

Prilla? Goose bumps erupted on Carol's arms. "Did she call Kane? Or did she show up?"

"She didn't call him often—Kane teased her a lot because she doesn't own a cell phone and uses pay phones. No, she came on the bus when he was still living with Darin, probably a month or two ago. Yeah, around Labor Day."

The visit may not have been recent, Carol thought, but it did show that Prilla and Kane were still connected.

"Darin got really mad when she stayed with them one night," the girl continued. "But Kane was happy she came. To tell you the truth, I think he liked his aunt way better than his mother. I'm not sure why he didn't live with her, but he did mention how he can't stand the cold up north." She dug her toe into the broken sidewalk. "He told me he hated his mom, but I knew he didn't mean it."

But what if he did? Carol stifled a shiver.

"Actually, I haven't seen Kane in weeks." A muscle worked in the girl's smooth, pale cheek. "I visited him when he was staying with a friend's family, but last I heard, he had moved on. Probably goes to the Feeding the Flock soup kitchen downtown when he gets hungry."

She said it matter-of-factly, as if Kane had ordered a burger in a drive-through. Though it was clear she was extremely young, the girl seemed so old, as if life had already put her through the wringer.

Resisting the urge to take the melancholy girl home with them and be kinder to her than anyone else apparently had been, Carol simply smiled. "Well, you've been a great help to us, and a good friend to Kane."

"If you see him, tell him Leia says hi."

"Will do."

A tiny smile budded on her thin lips. But she said nothing and headed back into the building.

Fighting the urge to follow, Carol fiddled with her phone. "The soup kitchen she mentioned isn't far from here. Let's check there first, then try Kristen's address."

Despite weekday traffic, it took little time to reach their destination. Once they parked, they followed signs to the Feeding the Flock dining room. Already, men, women, and children of all ages lined up for vegetable soup, chunks of bread, and fresh fruit.

Carol sniffed. "Mmm. Smells wonderful."

When the line of diners diminished, they asked one of the servers if she knew a teen boy named Kane Reed.

"Can't say that I do," the grandmotherly woman answered. "But I only volunteer on Tuesdays. Let me find somebody who's here all the time."

The lady returned a few minutes later with an older man who, despite his overall streetwise appearance, flashed a boyish smile. He introduced himself as Pete Gannon and said he helped with the affiliated men's shelter as well.

Pete settled them in a small, cluttered side office with foam cups of surprisingly good coffee. "I understand you're trying to find someone."

"Yes, Kane Reed," Carol answered. "He's in his teens, slim, with dark hair and light blue eyes. A friend of his told us he might be coming here for meals."

Pete didn't indicate whether he knew Kane or not. "Can you tell me why you're looking for this boy?"

At the shrewd note in Pete's pleasant voice, Carol explained about his mother's murder the previous week.

"That's horrible." Pete searched their faces. "Are you in law enforcement?"

"No." Harvey grasped Carol's hand. "At Kristen's funeral, my wife discovered that Kane might not know about her death. She found that unthinkable. She also cares deeply about his aunt, a suspect in the murder whom she believes is innocent."

"So you're trying to track down anything that might help the police find the real murderer—including whether it was Kane?" Pete obviously didn't mince words.

"That's about right," Carol told him.

"Well, I can tell you for sure that he didn't murder his mother," Pete said. "Kane was arrested and jailed a few weeks ago for robbing a convenience store."

Carol winced at the news. Kane was so young to be in such trouble.

"He's eighteen now, so he'll be tried as an adult." Pete sounded calm, but his big hand tightened around his cup.

"Do you know Kane well?" Carol asked.

"As well as anyone, I suppose. When he eats here, we talk cars. Occasionally, he'll open up a little and tell me how he's doing." He turned the question back on them. "Do you know Kane?"

"Not at all," Harvey told him.

"I know his aunt," Carol said. "Kane and Prilla appear to have something of a relationship. We heard she's visited him before. Has he mentioned anything about her coming recently?"

"No, but then, he wouldn't," Pete said. "Kane is all about protecting himself. He'd never admit bonding with anyone. Her name is Prilla?"

"Yes, Prilla Dunn. Short for Priscilla," Carol said. "Has she come here asking about him?"

"No," Pete answered firmly. "When Kane was arrested, he wouldn't give out information about relatives. We had hoped someone would show up here and ask about him." Pete cocked his head. "You're the only ones so far."

"I am surprised that Prilla hasn't attempted to tell Kane about his mother," Carol said. "I thought she might come here."

"Maybe she's too broke, or knew her truck wouldn't make it," Harvey suggested. "Or Prilla might be so scared that she's holed up someplace, hoping it will all go away."

Carol couldn't imagine Prilla intentionally letting Kane remain ignorant of his mother's death. Or letting him grieve alone.

She didn't want to think about the new man in Prilla's life, but if he cared for her, why hadn't he brought her to see Kane? Unless he didn't really care, but was simply exploiting her . . .

Birdie all over again.

Pete's quiet voice interrupted Carol's thoughts. "If you've never met Kane, then I should be the one who tells him about his mother. He'd think you were lined up with the police and would clam up so tightly, you couldn't open him with a crowbar."

"Understood," Harvey said.

"Besides," Pete continued, "even if Kane agreed to see you, I seriously doubt the people down at the juvenile detention center would allow it. They don't know you." A sad smile drifted across his face. "They do know me."

"I hate to dump this on you," Carol said hesitantly.

"I hate to have it dumped on me too. Passing along things like this never gets any easier." Pete gave them a rueful smile. "But I've had plenty of practice in breaking bad news to people, unfortunately. I'm pretty good at it." He reached over and patted her hand. "I'll do my best to help Kane through it. Everyone here"—he swept an arm to indicate the entire center—"will be praying for him."

"We will too. I'm so glad to know he has a healthy support system." Carol tried to keep tears from escaping.

"You bet," Harvey echoed.

Pete extended his hand. "We'll also pray that this murderer will be found, and that justice and mercy will be served."

"I'm praying for that as well," Carol said as she shook Pete's hand. "With all my heart."

Remembering the rude reception from Kane's former roommate, Carol hesitated before knocking at the apartment listed as Kristen's last known address. "Ready, Harvey?"

"If we wait for that, this conversation will never happen," he deadpanned.

The door creaked open with a groan and Carol nearly shook her head to clear her vision.

The man who answered was the spitting image of Elvis—if he'd lived to age 80 and let his hair go white. He leaned on a cane while two plump, black cats glared at the MacCallans from either side of his feet. "What can I do for you?"

"Um, hello." For the life of her, Carol couldn't think of anything else to say.

"Good morning," Harvey said. "I'm Harvey McCallan, and this is my wife, Carol. We have this as Kristen Reed's address."

A kaleidoscope of sadness, anger, hurt, and possibly love cast shadows over the man's lined face. "She lived here for a while, but I don't know where she is now."

"I'm afraid we do," Harvey said gently. "She passed away last week in Loch Mallaig. That's in the UP, where we live."

The old man's hand shook as he tried to steady himself. Then, fingering a tarnished cross on a gold chain around his neck, he asked hoarsely, "Was Kristen sick?"

Carol and Harvey hesitated, exchanging glances.

"Somebody finally killed her," the man muttered. "That's what happened, isn't it?"

"Yes," Carol said softly.

His shoulders sagged. "I knew it would happen someday. Just hoped I'd die before she did."

"Sir, can I get you a glass of water?" Carol offered. "Or call someone for you?"

"No need for that 'sir' business. The name's Norman." The man thumped the cane imperiously. "And there ain't anyone to call. Yet somehow, I always survive."

Carol wished she could ease Norman's obvious pain. "Maybe you should sit down for a little while," she suggested lamely.

Norman shrugged, but he waved a hand and said, "Come in." He limped to a dilapidated brown recliner in the middle of an equally derelict apartment. The cats settled into his lap, watching Carol and Harvey as if they were hostile intruders.

After fetching a glass of water, Carol and Harvey sat in the only other chairs they saw, which they retrieved from around a battered 1950s Formica table.

Their host hadn't raised his eyes since they entered. Now he muttered, "Have they caught whoever killed Kristen?"

"No," Harvey answered. "That's why we came to town. To track down her son and to learn more about Kristen so we can help find her killer."

The old man's bushy eyebrows shadowed his eyes. "Are you cops?"

Without going into detail about Prilla's relationship to Kristen, Carol explained that they were trying to help a friend suspected of her murder.

"Where you from again?" Norman demanded. When they reminded him, he muttered, "Must be some kind of a friend for you to come all the way down here."

Carol decided to shoot straight. "We need to know all we can about Kristen. Are you related to her somehow? Perhaps her father?"

"God help me, no." Norman stared straight through Carol. "She told me her dad was dead. But that probably was a lie, like half of what came out of her mouth." He leaned his head on his hand. "A couple of winters ago, I found Kristen downstairs in the front entry. Sick, skinny, looked like a frozen kitten. Shelters were full to overflowing. Couldn't just leave her there." Tears finally welled up in his aged eyes. "I came to regret that."

"I'm sorry," Carol said.

The man shifted in his chair. "If you're looking for that boy of hers, you might try Feeding the Flock downtown."

"I appreciate the suggestion, but we already went there." Harvey summarized their conversation with Pete.

"Those people are way too kind to that kid." Norman shook his head. "They were too kind to Kristen too."

Harvey squeezed Carol's hand. She sent him an appreciative smile as her husband's warmth had transfused into her, helping her get through this difficult morning.

He was also signaling that they needed to leave.

"We'd better go," she told Norman. "Can I fix you something to eat before we leave?"

"I appreciate it," he said. "But I don't really feel like eating right now."

Knowing grief could mask physical symptoms like hunger, Carol made a sandwich and opened a can of peaches she found in the near-empty cabinets. Often when she was too upset to eat, simply having food to eat nearby could spark her appetite after a while. "Promise me you'll eat this later today."

For the first time, a tiny twinkle lit Norman's eyes. "Bossy one, aren't you?"

"You don't know the half of it." Harvey assumed an air of martyrdom.

"Ah, you look like you're handling it pretty well." Norman leaned back in his chair. "You're both nice folks. Maybe too nice, like those soup kitchen people." His small grin faded.

"Maybe, but I'd rather be too nice than know I didn't help someone who might have needed it," Carol said gently. "I'm not responsible for how they use my help. I'm only responsible for giving it when I see someone who needs it. I don't know how Kristen hurt you, but I still think you did the right thing taking her in. Thanks for talking to us."

He gave a long, shuddering sigh. "I doubt I've been much help. Kristen used so many people and made so many enemies that I wonder if they'll ever find out who murdered her. Any one of a thousand could have done it."

10

How would Chief Thomson react when the MacCallans shared the results of their unsanctioned Benton Harbor trip? On the way home the previous day, Carol had tried to avoid the thought.

Sitting in his small, stark office, Carol waited for him to unleash the lecture that must be brewing in his mind as she said, "So Harvey and I checked out Benton Harbor, where Kristen Reed's last known address is."

Instead, touching his fingers together, the man simply looked tired.

"Chief?" Carol asked timidly.

"I'm sorry. It's just been a long week. We've had two burglaries, one at a convenience store and another at The Hamper. What did you get up to in Benton Harbor?"

Feeling even worse, Carol filled him in on everything she and Harvey had learned, grateful that her ever-supportive husband sat beside her.

When she was done, Thomson grimaced. "Kristen Reed's friend says she had a thousand enemies? I'm inclined to think he's right. The more we learn about her, the more we're adding to the list. I imagine some of her Benton Harbor connections might have hated her enough to follow her here."

Carol felt a thrill of relief that Prilla wasn't the department's only major suspect. That was one positive in this investigation. But why would one of Kristen's Benton Harbor acquaintances have drawn that ghoulish Celtic symbol on her? The reference to Matt Boersma's murder seemed to connect the killer to Loch Mallaig, but as far as Carol knew, he didn't have any connection to Kristen.

She tried to refocus on another somewhat positive fact. "At least we can take her son off the list."

"True," the chief said. "Her mother too. I confirmed that Lena Reed was in a Green Bay hospital at the time Kristen was murdered."

Upon learning Lena hadn't killed her daughter, Carol's heart leaped. A moment later, it sank. With Lena's exoneration, not to mention her close ties to several details of the crime, Prilla had moved up as a suspect once more.

So much for helping a friend. Carol leaned back in her chair, weary of it all.

"We also found Prilla's truck about forty miles from Marquette," the chief said. "Guessing it gave out on her. Country road, few houses, several miles from the interstate. No one who lives out there remembered seeing her."

"Knowing you were looking for her, it makes sense that she stayed off the beaten path," Harvey said.

"She also might have driven at night," Carol mused. "But if she broke down, how did she get to Marquette?"

"I understand she didn't carry a cell phone," Chief Thomson said. "Maybe Prilla walked to the nearest gas station to call her male companion, and he picked her up. Or perhaps she just walked the distance to the interstate and stuck out her thumb. Might even have met the man that way."

Carol really didn't want to think about that guy. If her friend had attached herself to the wrong kind of man . . .

A new, puzzled note in Chief Thomson's voice drew Carol back from her dark imaginings.

"Since Kristen Reed's murder appears to be connected, at least superficially, to Matt Boersma's twenty-five years ago, my officers and I have been sifting through every detail of both cases." The chief frowned. "We found something that doesn't make sense."

Prilla hadn't had anything to do with Matt's murder either, but Carol was eager to hear what the chief had to say.

"You've probably read in the paper that the knife that killed Boersma was found buried in the woods near the body," Thomson continued. "Well, the sheriff then, Don Lawrence, didn't test it for DNA or get a sample from Prilla. Just dusted the knife for fingerprints, which he reported were messy and inconclusive. DNA testing wasn't nearly as accurate as it is now, of course. Still, using it was routine procedure, especially in a serious crime like murder."

"Maybe Sheriff Lawrence simply made a mistake," Carol said. "Is he still around to ask?"

"Don died of cancer several years ago. I can't imagine him forgetting a major test like that." The chief shook his head. "He was a good friend of my father's, and I always looked up to him. Everyone did. Don was one reason I wanted to work in law enforcement."

Chief Thomson rarely displayed emotion, but Carol caught the muted turmoil in his voice.

Harvey must have too. "I'll bet there's some reasonable explanation for why the sheriff didn't test for DNA."

"Maybe." But it was obvious the chief didn't believe it.

"Is it possible to test the knife now?" Carol asked.

"We pulled it out of storage and sent it off this morning." Thomson's fingers tapped the desk, as if he couldn't wait for the results. "It won't be as accurate as if it had been done at the time of the murder. And the lab can only identify the killer if he's already in one of the databases. Still, it has to be done."

Who knew if the testing would link the two killings? DNA

results opened up all kinds of possibilities—some of which were not so good.

Carol bit her lip. Kristen and Prilla could have fought, especially when Kristen stole her locket. That didn't mean she'd killed her. Still, if they found Prilla and took a sample, the presence of Prilla's DNA on her dead half sister's body could make her look guiltier, especially in the eyes of the media. According to the comments below the latest articles Carol had read online, Prilla was still suspect number one in the gossip mill.

"So any foreign DNA found on Kristen's body is being tested too?" Carol asked.

"Of course," the chief answered. "We should hear back soon."

"The results might put some rumors to rest," Harvey said.

Carol hadn't thought of it in that positive way. This whole case was warping her perspective. She wilted in her chair, suddenly longing to take a trip somewhere that didn't involve murder.

Harvey touched her arm. "Let's go home, honey. We can stop on the way for a pumpkin spice latte. Then you can nap until your wedding cake appointment."

"I'd take the nap," Chief Thomson said. "And the latte. And I wouldn't say no to the cake either."

Carol laughed, and they said their goodbyes.

As she and Harvey walked to the car, she confided, "Molly doesn't know pumpkin spice lattes are my fall favorite."

He chuckled. "Don't worry. Your deep, dark secret is safe with me."

Later, sipping the spicy, creamy latte, Carol wished all secrets tasted as good as this one.

Wedding cakes were so fun to make.

As Harvey had predicted, the nap had refreshed Carol's positive attitude, and she was eager for her meeting with Sophia Hansen and Elijah Decker, who both taught with Jenny at the high school. Although their attire was sleek and trendy, they exuded an air of innocence as they joined Carol in the bakery office to discuss the cake for their wedding at the end of the month, since their original cake maker was no longer able to do it. Granted, they gazed at each other more often than they looked at the examples Carol was showing them, but Carol didn't mind young love at all. She and Harvey had probably behaved similarly when ordering their own cake.

Despite their starry-eyed distraction, they quickly chose their top five designs, then narrowed it down to their top three. When they selected their favorite with minimal back-and-forth, Carol mentally pegged them as a couple who would truly last until death did they part.

"Of course we'd like to customize the cake," Sophia said, turning bright eyes on Carol.

"Certainly." Carol always expected this. "We want this cake to be special. To be uniquely yours." She pointed to her suggested list of variations. "Would you prefer a different flavor of cake for each tier, or a different color frosting? Is there a particular flower you'd like me to include?"

"We like the colors and flowers as they are," Elijah said, "but both of us are strict vegans, so it just makes sense for us to have a vegan cake for our wedding. Can you do that?"

"Jenny mentioned that when she told me about you, so I prepared samples of the four vegan flavors I make," Carol said, pulling the dome off a cake stand where she'd arranged small slices of tester cakes. Baking a wedding cake without eggs or dairy presented more challenges than her usual recipes, especially in creating a light, delicate texture. She'd experimented for years, though, and prided herself on the delicious results.

Sophia and Elijah forked bites of each flavor into their mouths, they exclaimed over the taste of each one. After trying the last one, Sophia grew more serious. "I assume these are cruelty-free recipes? We feel we owe a special kindness to animals on our wedding day."

Cruelty-free? Carol couldn't remember having been asked that before. She'd used no eggs, milk, or butter. Hopefully, these two didn't consider beating the batter cruel.

"Do you cook meat in your kitchen?" Elijah asked before she'd had a chance to answer Sophia. "We prefer to avoid any contact with animal products."

"While we have used our oven for recipes containing meat in the past, Bread on Arrival doesn't serve anything but breads, pastries, and cakes," Carol informed him.

Her answer seemed to satisfy them. They discussed final details, then the couple put a deposit down on their cake. Carol was congratulating herself on having navigated tricky wedding cake waters when Sophia mentioned that she'd forgotten one more thing.

"Elijah and I are so glad that you understand our commitment to nature," Sophia said. "To emphasize our oneness with it, we want to replace the eight-inch tier of our wedding cake with an aquarium."

Carol paused. *Please,* please *say that I misheard you.*

"I found the perfect round one online," Sophia continued. "We'll bring our goldfish, Romeo and Juliet, a few days before the wedding, plus the aquarium supplies—"

She'd said it again. *Aquarium.*

Though a math teacher, Carol often had found herself cleaning neglected homeroom aquariums. Words like *slime, gunk,* and *flush* came to mind.

Words she couldn't bear to associate with a lovely, pristine wedding cake.

Carol opened her mouth to object, but the happy couple were already walking out the office door, confident they'd checked off one more item on their wedding to-do list.

For some minutes, she simply sat. Then she went downstairs in search of sympathetic ears—and chocolate. Down in the kitchen, she told Laura and Molly, who had begun after-hours cleaning, about her newest wedding cake adventure.

"Well, give them credit," Laura said. "They didn't ask you to top it with their pet guinea pigs."

Carol didn't feel particularly grateful. She went to the walk-in freezer, retrieved the luscious dark chocolate-caramel torte she'd stored there last week, and fired up the coffee machine.

Instead of waiting for her creation to thaw, she carved off a healthy slice of it and plopped it onto a plate. "Okay, this is my share—for now. How much do you two want?"

Laura and Molly piped up that they too warranted large chunks, due to the stresses of keeping up with production without her. Carol agreed.

They sat around a prep table, devouring cake and sipping coffee, too engrossed in their therapy to talk much. Finally, nothing remained but a last sliver of the torte.

Carol realized they all were eying its moist, chocolatey goodness as if it were their last hope. Assuming a noble air, she said, "As partners forever, we should split this equally."

Molly and Laura offered no objection.

They were polishing off the last crumbs when Hamish, who had been winterizing the bakery and its grounds, entered. To Carol's relief, he made no smart remarks about their snack. "Ah, it's good to see you three together again. This bakehouse, like the universe, needs a trinity to run smoothly."

He handed them their stack of mail. Molly, who handled most of the office work, dug through it.

"Anything exciting?" Carol cast a glance at the pile.

"Bills, junk mail, the usual . . . what's this?" She held a small, sealed manila envelope with *Bread on Arrival* typed on the front.

"No address or stamp," Laura observed.

"Might be thank-you notes." Carol smiled. "Remember when the third-grade teacher dropped off those cute little letters after we gave them a tour?"

"Sure, but I can't think of anyone who'd be sending us notes now." Molly slit the envelope and removed the contents. "It's a newspaper clipping."

Molly unfolded the paper.

Carol froze, and Hamish uttered a sharp exclamation in Gaelic that needed no translation.

The article, published when the bakehouse had first opened, featured a photo of the partners smiling on the front porch. A heavy, black symbol had been drawn across Carol's smiling face.

Molly quavered, "I've seen that before somewhere, but I can't remember what it means—"

"I know what it means." Hamish's face had tightened into a grim mask. "It's the Celtic symbol for death."

11

"Stay safe," Chief Thomson had told them in lieu of goodbye when Carol had called to report the clipping's not-so-veiled threat. Like Carol, he couldn't believe Prilla would have sent such nasty mail. Perhaps the man she was with had snuck it into the mailbox, or Kristen's killer was feeling the heat and had sent a warning shot.

Staying safe was easier said than done when Prilla was still missing and a murderer was on the loose, but Carol didn't mind keeping close to home. She'd had enough of chasing down Kristen's relatives. One aspect of the case remained that she hadn't explored, but at least she wouldn't have to leave town to do it.

"Prilla's basically a homebody," Carol said to her partners as they grabbed supper at Neeps and Tatties. "I'll bet that after the Marquette trip, she returned to this area."

Molly cocked her head. "Are you going to search for her?"

Carol plunged her fork into the hot, buttered neeps and potatoes beside the roast beef on her plate. "I think it makes sense since she's still the police's primary suspect."

She didn't say aloud that despite the reported sightings, she couldn't shake the mental alarms that urged her to find Prilla as quickly as possible. And that she couldn't shake an increasingly bad feeling about Prilla's male companion . . .

Laura's no-nonsense voice focused Carol again. "The police have been looking for Prilla for days. They haven't found her."

Carol dropped the fork beside her plate. "I still have to do this."

"But how will you do it and stay safe?" Laura challenged.

"Maybe we can make this search a little safer." Molly leaned forward. "I'll go too, and we'll ask Fergus to go with us. And I assume Harvey will come?"

"I haven't drafted him yet." Carol half chuckled. "But I doubt he'll let me go beating the bushes to find an accused murderer without him."

"A group of four might prove safer than wandering by yourself in the woods," Laura admitted, "though I'd feel better if you were armed."

"To search for Prilla?" Carol stared at her partner. "That's like taking a rifle to look for a lamb."

"Prilla wouldn't shoot you," Laura flung back, "but the nut who sent that clipping might."

True. Carol's skin prickled. Still, she insisted, "Harvey and I survived searching for Kane with only our wits. We can do the same in this situation."

Laura muttered something about moving back to New York to stay safe, but Carol knew she'd won her skeptical friend over when she offered to call Bridget and the Bruces to help work their shifts.

Molly was already on the phone with Fergus. Carol, who knew Harvey's calendar was open, texted him to confirm. They all agreed to search for Prilla the next morning.

With her plan set in motion, Carol's insides knotted. Rising a little unsteadily from her seat, she wished the others a good night, then drove home with the same two questions repeating in her mind.

Would they find Prilla? More importantly, would they find her safe?

"Dad, we're not interfering with the police investigation." Fergus, standing at the other end of the bakehouse's front porch with his phone to his ear, cast a beleaguered frown at Carol, Harvey, and Molly. "We're just volunteers who want this nightmare to end."

After several attempts to end the conversation, Fergus finally said a firm goodbye and pocketed his phone. "Wish Dad had gone to Arizona," he muttered as he rejoined them. "Or maybe the moon." To Fergus's dismay, his father had decided to delay going to Arizona until, as he put it, "the current crisis is solved."

Poor guy, Carol thought with a smile. He seemed to alternate between worrying about his father and wanting to muzzle him. She sent up a pray of thanks that, even in her eighties, her own mother, Mimi, was more easygoing than Gordon.

As they walked to Fergus's Range Rover, Carol watched Molly try to lighten his mood. Carol laid a mental bet that he'd smile well before they reached Prilla's.

She was right, but all their smiles faded as they approached the cabin.

The beautiful fall morning should have inspired optimism. As they pulled into the cabin's overgrown driveway, though, Carol found herself trying to push away memories of when she and Laura had visited Prilla's abandoned home only days ago.

Professionals had already searched this area. Carol and company didn't know Prilla well, so how could they find her favorite spots in this forest? What could they hope to accomplish?

Be quiet, Carol told her doubts.

Though they all owned smartphones, she handed out maps of the area. "In the search and rescue articles I've been reading, they emphasize teamwork. I wish we could do a slow search for clues, but we don't have that much time." She pointed to the zones she'd numbered on the maps. "If each of us takes a section, we could cover a fairly large area by noon."

The zones in question hardly put a dent in the land between Prilla's cabin and the Lake Superior shore, but they had to start somewhere.

Harvey, who had wanted Carol to search with him, frowned. But rather than argue, he simply urged everyone to keep their phones handy. "Stay paranoid. Thank goodness reception's decent out here. Let's text each other every hour. And if you see *any*thing suspicious, no matter how minor it may seem, call the others."

Everyone donned orange vests borrowed from Castleglen, as archery deer-hunting season had begun. They conducted final backpack checks.

"Everybody have leather gloves?" Harvey asked. "Sharp clippers? I've heard some of these paths are nearly impassable. I brought a small hatchet if someone needs it."

"So did I." Fergus zipped his backpack, then scanned his phone, his expression darkening. "Dad called again."

Molly touched his arm. "But didn't you say that you asked Neil to check on him and your mother?"

"Yeah, and if it's urgent, he'll call Neil." Fergus turned off his screen. "I just wish he'd quit harping on this murder case."

Carol watched as Fergus shouldered his backpack, wondering about Gordon's obsession. Everyone else apparently chalked it up to age. Still, a tiny wheel turned in Carol's mind: Had Gordon seen something related to Kristen's killing that had made him afraid? If so, why wouldn't he have said something?

Harvey's brisk, no-nonsense voice brought her back to the present. "All right, ready to head out?"

"Not yet," Carol said. "We need major help on this search. Let's pray."

They grasped hands, and she led a short prayer.

Then she handed out still-warm baps with cinnamon butter. "Prilla's favorite Tuesday morning treat. Let's do this for her."

Munching the baps, the group scattered, but not before Harvey caught her hand, warned her to be safe, and planted a quick kiss on her forehead. Carol headed into her zone, the one nearest Lake Superior. Thank goodness for high boots. The unusually lovely October weather meant snakes probably hadn't yet hibernated.

Had anyone reported seeing bears lately?

Carol pushed the thoughts away, choosing instead to focus on the sun-dappled, leaf-covered ground. Her gaze swept the undergrowth for broken twigs or torn branches that might suggest someone else had passed this way. Thankful for her thick, sturdy clothing, she pushed through tangled vines and thorny thickets. Occasional foam cups and torn snack packaging aroused her irritation at careless hikers, but nothing suspicious turned up. Soon, Harvey's anxious texts every thirty minutes morphed into *OK?* and *Good* at wider spaced intervals.

At noon, the searchers met to wolf down their lunches near a small pasture bordered by one of the few paved roads.

They talked and laughed to cover lack of success. Under her own chatter, Carol doggedly clung to her resolve. She'd search as long as she needed to find Prilla and bring her safely home. However, once she sat, Carol's legs didn't want to move. Though active, she didn't spend hours at a time hiking through untamed wilderness. Carol wobbled when she tried to stand.

"Grab a few winks with me." Harvey, leaning against a big maple, pulled her down beside him. "You'll feel stronger if you do."

She wanted to resist, but his arm felt so good around her . . .

The roar of a passing truck woke Carol from deep slumber. With a start, she sat up. "What time is it?"

"Don't panic." Harvey yawned as he checked his watch. "We only napped for about twenty minutes. Hardly long enough to call it sleep."

Fergus and Molly, who had been chatting together on a nearby log, turned their attention to the MacCallans. "Hey there, sleepyheads," Molly said.

"We were about to poke you with a stick," Fergus joked.

"You're just jealous," Carol replied with a grin. "I feel loads better." Climbing to her feet, she pulled the map from her pocket. "Let's get our new zones straight so we can move out."

They picked their areas and set out with renewed energy.

Carol shoved aside saplings and curtains of grapevines blocking her path. She yanked free from the clutches of thorny vines, searching for anything that might reveal Prilla's presence.

Even the traces of trash disappeared as she pushed deeper into Oppen Woods.

Trying to make her way sideways through a clump of seemingly impassable thickets, Carol smacked against a hard surface. Rubbing her hip, she realized she hadn't struck a sapling. She'd hit something flat. Carol thrust her gloved hands into the mass of gnarly vegetation and felt disintegrating boards held together with knobby nails. It was a building, barely taller than Carol.

Was it a deer stand? If so, the owner must be quite short. Maybe it was just a chicken coop, abandoned long ago.

A rusty screech split the afternoon as a door opened. An equally rusty voice with an oddly familiar note spoke. "Who are you? And why are you at my door?"

12

A tiny figure in faded, mismatched clothes guarded the door of the vine-covered hut.

Carol stared, speechless. Had she stumbled into a fairy tale?

Squinting, she recognized Blanche Geller, the friend Prilla had brought with her to Bread on Arrival. She watched Carol with wary eyes.

"Hi, Blanche." She spoke gently. "I'm Carol MacCallan. My partners and I own a bakery in town. Do you remember coming in with Prilla for baps?"

"Baps?" The piquant, wrinkly face rearranged into a thoughtful expression.

"Hot, buttered rolls. Prilla bought you one when you visited a few weeks ago."

Blanche's face broke into the childlike smile Carol remembered. "That was a good roll. The dog was nice too."

Thank goodness Angus had welcomed Blanche with open paws. Carol grabbed the positive moment to glean information. "Have you seen Prilla since then?"

The woman's smile faded. "Prilla walks in the night. I don't like the night."

"I'd rather walk during the day too," Carol said. "Isn't it a beautiful day?"

Instead of answering, Blanche pivoted abruptly. She gestured to Carol, who hesitated. Should she text Harvey before entering? Her hand slid into her jacket pocket for her phone and her keys, which she could use for defense in a pinch.

For crying out loud, Carol. This woman hardly comes up to your belly button. Releasing her keys, she ducked through the doorway and followed Blanche into the fairy-tale hut, where a dented copper kettle whistled atop a small woodstove.

Though primitive, the one-room house appeared tidy. The rough table held a jar with sprigs of red-orange bittersweet berries. They caught a sunbeam from a single window, half-covered by vines. Blanche took two chipped but clean mugs from a near-empty shelf, and loose tea and strainers from a battered wooden box that apparently served as a cabinet. Pouring hot water from the kettle, she motioned to a backless bench at the table.

Carol sat, grateful for the chance to rest and hoping this visit would provide more than a brief respite from her search.

Blanche brought the steaming mugs and sat beside her. They sipped the fragrant brew. Carol decided to let Blanche break the silence.

What she said next almost made Carol choke on her tea.

"Sometimes I wonder if Prilla is a faerie." Blanche's thin shoulders hunched under her shapeless dress.

"Prilla's not a faerie," Carol answered calmly. "She's a woman like you and me."

"But she walks the night. She comes from bad blood."

Carol froze. At Kristen's funeral, Lena had said the same thing about her daughter. "What makes you say that, Blanche? Prilla is your friend, isn't she?"

"Yes. She's my friend. She brings me food." The corners of Blanche's mouth twisted down. "But she has bad blood. Prilla walks the night with the cursed faeries and brings food to them. To the ghosts too."

Even as Carol's patience ebbed, a tingle of fear crawled up her spine. "She isn't a cursed faerie, Blanche. She may need help. Where is Prilla? Can you tell me?"

"She walks the night. She walks to the big water."

"Lake Superior?" At least Carol had been heading the right direction. Maybe.

"Yes. Didn't tell the big men. Didn't want them to find Prilla."

"Big men?" Carol prodded her brain anew. A picture of tall Chief Thomson and Deputy Chief Broderick Gillespie in uniform rose in her mind. "The police?"

Blanche's face went white before she dropped her chin to her chest and hunched her shoulders even more.

Carol cringed at the response. "Blanche? I'm sorry. I didn't mean to upset you."

Blanche didn't reply. Carol tried alternating silence with gentle coaxing, but the other woman remained unresponsive.

After checking her phone for the time, Carol realized she couldn't stay any longer. "Thanks for the cup of tea, Blanche. I'm Prilla's friend. I hope you'll consider me yours too."

A slight movement told Carol the woman had heard and understood. Still, she remained with her head down as Carol left.

Once outside, Carol couldn't text the others fast enough, telling them briefly about finding Blanche and taking a new direction. They agreed to meet at a nearby pond.

Harvey arrived first at a dead run. He skidded to a stop in front of Carol and grasped her upper arms, examining her closely. "Are you okay?"

Carol laughed. "Blanche is half my size. I'm fine."

Molly soon emerged from the woods, with Fergus getting there a few minutes later. Carol summarized her visit with Blanche. "Sometimes she almost made sense, then she'd start talking nonsense about faeries. I wonder how well she gets by, living alone out in the woods."

"Sounds like she's got Prilla checking on her," Fergus said. "Though with Prilla missing, there's more to be concerned about."

Molly voiced the question that had been floating through Carol's mind. "Why would Prilla walk to the lake at night? Blanche said that several times, didn't she?"

Carol tapped her chin. "I think we have to take that much at face value, though I can't imagine Prilla braving this terrain in the dark."

"She grew up in these woods, though, didn't she?" Harvey noted.

"She did," Carol confirmed. Prilla probably knew every path, every tree and thicket. "She must have told Blanche about her nighttime hikes—with Blanche's fear of the dark, I doubt that she joined her, but maybe Prilla stopped by Blanche's on her way to the lake. She did say Prilla brought her food."

"But why would she say Prilla took food to faeries and ghosts?" Harvey shook his head. "Just how much of her story should we believe?"

"There might be more to the ghost thing than we realize." Fergus frowned. "I remember when I was a kid there was talk about a lighthouse on a little overgrown peninsula that jutted into Lake Superior."

Molly cocked her head. "What's that got to do with Blanche's faeries and ghosts?"

"Everyone thought it was haunted," Fergus said. "The story was that sometime during the late 1800s, the lightkeeper had it in for the captain of a certain ship because he'd led his daughter astray. One stormy night, when the keeper knew that ship was passing nearby, he extinguished the light, causing not only that ship to go down, but one other." Fergus lowered his voice and adopted a Scottish brogue, which Carol had to admit leant a fine ambience to the tale. "Because of his sins, the lightkeeper turned into the most evil of faeries, wreaking havoc on anyone he could. Some say he still roams the shoreline, but every night, he must return to the lighthouse. One can hear the groans of the keeper as he is tormented forever by the ghosts of the ships' lost captains and sailors. Anyone who tries to rescue him dies by their hand."

After he finished, his audience remained silent. The creepy tale seemed to have cast a spell over them all.

Molly broke it with a loud snort. "Good grief, Fergus. As if we don't have enough real scary stories around here without digging up fake ones."

"Do people really avoid that lighthouse because they think it's haunted?" Carol asked.

"You'd better believe it," Fergus said in his normal voice. "I only saw it once. I kept a good distance—and not just because of the lightkeeper legend. When I was in school, I researched the UP's lighthouses and came across an interesting newspaper story from the 1950s. It reported that a group of teens dared approach the 'haunted' one. Only one boy—a bright, happy kid, according to his buddies—climbed to the top. They insisted he didn't stand on the walkway because it didn't look strong enough to hold his weight. Yet his friends watched as he fell and died on the rocks below." Fergus shuddered. "Still, no one found evidence of foul play. Since then, even the police avoid that lighthouse."

"Thanks so much for *that* story too." Molly shook her head. "Don't we all feel so much safer?"

"Actually, I'm glad you told it," Carol countered, "because what if Prilla headed for the lighthouse? It would be a great place to hide if no one else will go anywhere near it. She might have taken along some food for herself. If Blanche saw her, she easily could have thought Prilla was taking food to the faeries." Carol glanced around their small circle. "Do you think we should check it out?"

Silence hung over the group until Harvey harrumphed. "I can see you're going. So I guess that means that I am too."

"I'm game." Molly seemed a little frightened, but she cast a teasing glance at Fergus. "And you, oh great storyteller?"

"As if I'd miss this." Fergus lifted his chin. "But I think it wise to use caution. For one thing, that lighthouse is well over a century old. Falling through rotten floors isn't going to help us solve this case."

"That's true," Carol said. "If it appears unsafe, let's just take a preliminary peek around. Who knows? We may find Prilla, or at least indications that she's been there. If nothing turns up, we can search the woods between there and Blanche's hut until dark."

"Sounds like a plan." Fergus pulled out his map. The lighthouse wasn't labeled, but he pointed to a spot near the lake. "The building may have fallen apart since I was a kid. But here's the peninsula where it was located."

They all donned their backpacks again and headed that way.

Hiking together was much more fun than searching alone. They were able to talk and laugh, while moving faster because they had four pairs of eyes searching rather than only one.

Bushes along the way often held broken branches and twigs. Made by deer or elk? A human? A bear?

Carol examined another small, broken branch on the ground. She and Molly exchanged tentative glances. "I've heard most bears are more afraid of us than we are of them," Carol said with forced bravado.

"I hope so," Molly muttered.

In a muddy area, Carol spied what appeared to be men's footprints and took photos. "These could be Prilla's. She wore those big boots sometimes. But they could be a hunter's too."

After more than an hour of hiking, their search for clues almost morphed into a game. Carol nearly forgot Fergus's eerie lighthouse tales.

When he halted in his tracks and pointed, though, their merry conversation ceased. They couldn't yet see Lake Superior, but the relentless sound of waves devouring the rocks echoed in their silence.

Carol's mouth went dry.

Peering over half-dead pine trees, blank windows watched them from a ruined tower, ringed near the top by a slumping walkway. As they crept closer, taking care to keep under cover, a small house attached to the tower came into view. Overgrown and missing many bricks, it sagged as if weighed down by secrets.

No wonder everyone avoids this place. Even in broad daylight, Carol shuddered.

Would Prilla have approached this lighthouse at night? Only survival instinct could have prompted anyone to do that, though at the moment Carol's was screaming at her to stay away from it.

A notice had been posted beside the front door. Carol strained her eyes, trying to read the large print at the top.

Fergus's vision trumped hers. He whispered, "It says to keep out. The lighthouse is owned by the state."

One part of Carol was swamped with relief that they wouldn't have to enter. The other part wanted to ignore the sign and check it out anyway.

She had to remind herself that her goal was to find Prilla and send a murderer to jail, not go there herself.

"For now, let's look around outside," she said, matching Fergus's low tone. "Harvey, let's check the south side. Molly and Fergus, would you scout the north side? Keep out of sight. We'll meet back here."

They split up. Harvey, whose research for wildlife magazine articles had taught him something about forest stealth, could slip through thickets and briars with minimal injury. Carol, on the other hand, had to press her lips together when thorns pierced her light jacket. Noticing her flinches, Harvey grabbed bushes and branches so she could pass through unhurt, yet keep an eye on the lighthouse, which seemed completely deserted. When they almost had to crawl through a wall of prickly growth, Harvey braved it first, creating a path for her to follow.

They made it into a more open area, which might have been a small pasture or vegetable garden once upon a time. Carol welcomed the break as viewing the lighthouse was much easier here, but finding cover was more difficult. Fortunately, a tumbledown shed aided their efforts.

Carol strained her ears, trying to detect any hints of voices, music, or anything else that might indicate human life nearby. No movement interrupted the emptiness of cracked windows. Not a single candy bar wrapper or empty water bottle indicated the presence of humans. Perhaps that in itself was suspicious? Surely other hikers, perhaps even ghost hunters who had heard Fergus's story, had visited during the past months.

If they could examine the ground around the lighthouse for footprints, perhaps they'd find some that matched the ones she'd photographed in the woods. Drawing closer, Carol noticed a small, rickety dock with an equally ramshackle boathouse behind the lighthouse. Had someone concealed a skiff among the rocks or inside the boathouse?

We can't solve anything by prowling outside. More than ever, Carol chafed at their limited search. At this point, a better alternative would be to return as quickly as possible to talk to Chief Thomson.

Did the police still avoid the lighthouse, as Fergus had implied? None of them had been around during the 1950s. Still, spooky legends often endured for generations. This one seemed firmly entrenched in local lore.

Even if the police had already searched the lighthouse, she'd tell them about Blanche's strange reference to Prilla's nocturnal hikes.

Perhaps they'd investigate it again. Chief Thomson could certainly gain legal access to the lighthouse much quicker than they could.

Meanwhile, Carol hoped Molly and Fergus had found something. She whispered to Harvey that they should go back to their meeting place, and he nodded. She was tempted to suggest circumventing the briar patch, but with a sigh, she followed their original route, which gave them a closer view. She kept her gaze locked on the lighthouse, but she still didn't see a flicker of movement.

When they returned to their rendezvous point, Fergus and Molly were waiting, and both signaled a thumbs-down.

Carol motioned for them all to leave. The group, still scanning the area for clues, hiked a quarter mile or so back into the woods, then stopped to compare notes.

"I'm so frustrated." Carol gulped from her water bottle. "I want to run back to Loch Mallaig and talk to Chief Thomson about the lighthouse. But at the same time, I'd like to slow down and search this section more thoroughly." She didn't dare look at Harvey as she said, "Actually, I'd like to come back tonight. That's when Blanche said Prilla roams the woods."

"Not on your life." Harvey crossed his arms. "Wander around here at night when there's a murderer loose? That's insane."

"I'm with Harvey." Molly scowled at Carol. "Have you forgotten about the nut who sent us that clipping?"

Although more polite about saying it, Fergus agreed with Harvey and Molly. "Remember, we're basing these suspicions on Blanche's word. While she may be accurate about some things, she doesn't seem to have her wits entirely about her."

"Okay, okay." Carol jumped to her feet and donned her backpack again. "Let's hurry back to town and talk to the chief. He may know more about the lighthouse than we think he does."

Even though she couldn't see it from where they were, Carol couldn't help glancing over her shoulder toward the lighthouse as they left. Were the answers they all searched for right there, so close and yet still out of reach?

13

A clearly exhausted Chief Thomson was just leaving when Carol and Harvey arrived at the station, but he stopped to chat with them anyway. Upon hearing that they had been searching for Prilla with Molly and Fergus, who had gone home, his expression hardened. "Is this your idea of staying safe?"

Carol winced but kept her voice strong. "We figured we were as safe together in the woods as we would have been in town." Though the chief definitely didn't look like he'd welcome hearing about Blanche or the haunted lighthouse, she decided to tell him anyway. She described her encounter with Blanche, then asked, "Did any of your officers mention questioning her?"

"This sounds like the same little old lady who muttered something about walking in the dark—it was daytime— then slammed her door in our faces," the chief answered. "We didn't want to scare her. We also didn't think she'd be much help, so we left. The next day, I called senior services to see if they could give her a hand."

"That was good of you," Carol said. She explained about Blanche's references to Prilla's nighttime hikes. She hesitated briefly, then related the woman's supernatural hints that had steered them toward the lighthouse as Prilla's possible hiding place.

No doubt Chief Thomson often listened to odd clues from "helpful" townspeople without flinching. Tonight, however, he rubbed his receding hairline wearily. "After finding Kristen Reed's body, my officers and I, plus volunteers, searched the entire area between Prilla Dunn's cabin and Lake Superior, which included that lighthouse. No one reported anything unusual."

"I see." Carol appreciated his not dismissing her and her friends outright. However, she couldn't accept that their search today had been unwarranted. Were they missing something? "Is there any news at all about Kristen's case, Chief?"

"I can tell you that it's doubtful she was killed by someone responsible for the other murders that have happened in the region recently," he answered. "The murder in Copper Harbor involved a family grudge, and the L'Anse killing also appears unrelated to Kristen's case. I doubt that will calm things in Loch Mallaig, but one can hope."

He said it with such weariness that Carol took pity on him. "We do appreciate the hard work you and your officers do. I simply want to help my friend."

"I know," the chief said, his tone softening. "I appreciate your community spirit and dedication. I'll let you know when any new developments surface."

With that, Carol and Harvey found themselves outside Loch Mallaig Town Hall, shivering a little, as the sun had just gone down.

Harvey's arm encircled her. "Come on, honey. Let's go home."

Rubber legs threatening to collapse, Carol realized the visit to Chief Thomson had drained the last drop of energy from her reservoir. She felt a jolt of gratitude for Harvey's support, both emotional and physical. The jolt amped up to a surge when Carol walked through their front door and was met by the rich, savory fragrance of beef stew wafting from the kitchen.

"Figured we'd be hungry this evening," Harvey explained. "So I asked Jenny to stop by and put some dinner in the slow cooker."

"You're a prince among men, Harvey MacCallan," Carol said sincerely. "And Jenny's not so bad either."

After supper, Harvey checked a text. "Huh," he said, then turned off the screen.

"What is it?" Carol asked.

"Nothing." But he answered too quickly.

"Harvey."

"Okay, okay." Harvey held up his hands to gesture surrender. "My buddy scored an extra ticket to that outdoors journalism conference on Mackinac Island this weekend."

Carol blinked. "I thought you were really disappointed when it was sold out and you couldn't go."

"I was. And this is a great opportunity." He rubbed the back of his neck. "Problem is, I'd have to leave early tomorrow morning and wouldn't be back for a couple of days." Harvey fixed concerned eyes on her. "With all that's going on right now, I don't want to be away from you."

She didn't particularly relish the prospect herself, but she couldn't keep him away from something he'd wanted as much as this, especially with how extra-wonderful he'd been lately. "Of course you should go. This is a great organization, one you've wanted to be part of for a long time, right? People you've always wanted to meet?"

"Well, yeah—"

"Then tell your friend that you'll do it. Now, before he finds somebody else to take your ticket." She tapped his phone pointedly.

"Yes ma'am," Harvey said with mock deference.

While Harvey texted his friend, Carol changed into pajamas and got ready for bed. Although her body demanded sleep, Harvey needed the bedroom lights on so he could pack. It was just as well since her mind had no intention of closing down. Ideas flooded unbidden into her head.

She went to the living room with her laptop. Sitting in front of the fire, Carol opened her computer. First, she wanted to delve into the haunted lighthouse's history. Then, if her brain still wouldn't allow for sleep, she'd find out more about both Prilla and Kristen.

Carol didn't discover much new information about the lighthouse online, but she found enough to corroborate the facts behind the legend Fergus had related. Built in 1886, the lighthouse had served the area for a decade before inexplicably failing one night, causing two shipwrecks. The lightkeeper, a widower who lived alone after sending a teen daughter to live with relatives in Petoskey, had disappeared and was never seen again.

Fergus had also accurately remembered the details of the teen boy's fall from the lighthouse in the 1950s. No one ever determined exactly how the incident had happened, though the police unofficially considered it an accident. They had believed the boy's companions, who gave matching, detailed accounts. No motives had ever surfaced for their involvement in foul play.

Carol did find one reference to the rumors of the lighthouse being haunted. Many state-owned lighthouses in the UP had been restored, often with local residents contributing to the cause. Because Loch Mallaig and surrounding areas viewed this one as haunted, the state was not able to raise sufficient funds to improve it.

Having exhausted that subject for now, Carol hesitated. If she searched either Priscilla Dunn or Kristen Reed, all the lurid media accounts of Kristen's murder would spray across her screen. Yet with Blanche mentioning Prilla's "bad blood," she simply had to dig into their background.

For now, she'd stick to public records. Fortunately, several of the UP's counties had listed birth, death, and marriage records online. To Carol's surprise, she discovered that Prilla Dunn had been born Priscilla Rose Nilson on March 19, 1979, the daughter of Kathryn

Dunn Nilson and Mark Nilson. Not long after, however, her mother had divorced her father and reverted to her maiden name, Dunn. She had legally changed her young daughter's last name as well.

But if Prilla and Kristen had the same father, why did Kristen also bear her mother's name rather than Nilson?

According to public records, Lena Reed had never been married, and she'd chosen to give Kristen her own last name from her birth, which had been in 1980.

With two sets of mothers and daughters rejecting his name, Mark Nilson must have been a piece of work. Carol decided to plug his name into a search engine.

Gradually, as she applied filters, arrests from across the country popped up—repeated charges of petty theft, reckless driving, and failure to pay child support. Something else nagged at Carol's mind, though. She'd seen or heard Mark Nilson's name before, but when? Where? Her mind spun and the links listed on the screen blurred, then disappeared, then reappeared . . .

"Carol, you're falling asleep," Harvey said gently. "We both need to go to bed."

He was right, as usual. She'd pursue this in the morning before her shift at the bakehouse. Carol powered down the laptop, stumbled into their bedroom, and collapsed onto the nice, soft bed.

She immediately fell asleep, but her brain refused to rest. In dream after dream, she came within a hair's breadth of discovering the elusive truth she was seeking, only to lose it like water vapor through her fingers. In one vivid dream, the potbellied man from Kristen's funeral was waltzing Prilla across a frozen pond and into a waiting police car. In another, Carol climbed stair after crumbling stair inside a lighthouse, never falling but never able to make any progress toward the top.

Before dawn the next morning, she heard Harvey in the kitchen and forced her groggy body out of bed and into the hallway. As she walked to the kitchen, she glared at her laptop, which was resting on the living room coffee table.

Harvey, who obviously had been up for a while, followed her gaze and handed her a giant mug of coffee. "Sure you can't go back to bed for a few minutes?"

"I have to go to work," Carol grumbled.

"Well, I hope you have a light day." He pulled her to him for a big hug. "I fed the chickens, but I have to take off."

She'd told him to go to Mackinac Island, but that didn't make it easy to kiss him goodbye and watch his Jeep head off down the road. She usually took his trips in stride, even enjoyed having the house to herself. But Harvey was right. Prilla's disappearance, Kristen's murder, the difficult trips to Marquette and Benton Harbor—not to mention the clipping with the Celtic death symbol—all made her feel vulnerable.

And alone. Very alone.

Carol shook herself. *What's your problem, girl? You'll see him again before you know it.*

Besides, this was an excellent opportunity to eat some of the instant oatmeal that was her guilty pleasure. Harvey, who preferred a big breakfast, always turned up his nose at it. She quickly microwaved herself a bowl, then made a mental list of to-dos before work: feed Pascal, write up a grocery list, gather all the old newspapers and put out the recycling—

A lightning bolt lit her brain. *That's it.*

She'd seen Mark Nilson's name in the *Crown Press News*.

Carol dumped some food in the cat's bowl, then hurried to her laptop. She scrolled and scanned the Mark Nilson search engine results again. She opened an article from a Detroit paper, much more extensive than what she remembered in her hometown paper.

"Yes!" Carol pumped her fist.

Last spring, Nilson, under the alias Marshall Hale, had bilked investors out of more than a million dollars. So far, the police hadn't been able to find him.

Carol clasped her hands and said aloud, "I bet I know where he is. The lighthouse."

In her mind, she could hear skeptical Harvey's protests about how the place had looked deserted. But it had been *too* deserted yesterday, like a pistol wiped clean of fingerprints. And Blanche had rambled about Prilla taking food to cursed faeries . . .

Nilson had been hiding at the lighthouse, all right. And he'd conned his daughter into helping him. Maybe he was scheming an escape to Canada.

Carol's stomach lurched with another realization. The guy in a hoodie at the convenience store was Prilla's father, not a boyfriend or someone she'd met when her truck broke down.

Unbelievable. Nilson's behavior was so unlike Harvey's, who loved and protected Jenny with all his heart. So different from Carol's own caring father. Neither of them would ever dream of putting their daughters in a dangerous situation.

Carol clenched her fists. Maybe he'd already taken Prilla—more a prisoner than a daughter from the looks of it—to Canada.

But what if he hadn't wanted her along? A greedy criminal like Nilson would put himself above everyone, even his own children. The more people who knew where he was, the more likely he'd end up in jail. So how would he ensure his safety?

Eliminate those who knew where he was.

Carol choked on her breath.

Maybe he'd already killed Kristen, and Prilla was next on his list.

How Carol longed to call Harvey and hear his sane, gentle voice telling her she was jumping to conclusions. But he would make a U-turn, come home to her, and miss the conference he so wanted to attend.

She couldn't let that happen, so she'd call Chief Thomson instead. That's what Harvey would want her to do anyway.

But the overworked chief had barely tolerated her last night. If she charged into his office spouting unsolicited help yet again, he might discount anything she told him simply because he was tired of her interference.

Carol told herself to sit and breathe for a while, to let her thoughts settle into some semblance of reasonable order. She'd call Chief Thomson later, after he'd had his morning coffee—but not too long after. As more hours passed, the likelihood of finding Prilla would continue to shrink.

She sank onto the sofa in front of the fire. Pascal, who usually exhibited no sensitivity to her feelings whatsoever, padded over and rubbed against her legs briefly before wandering to the kitchen for his breakfast.

She certainly hadn't intended to fall asleep, but she must have, because the housephone ringing woke her. She rose and stumbled to the kitchen, where she picked up the receiver. "Hello?"

"Carol?"

Carol jerked awake. "Prilla, are you all right? Where are you?"

"I—I'm at the haunted lighthouse." Her soft voice quavered like a child's. "The one near the lake."

"I know where it is." Carol gripped the phone. "Are you okay?"

"I'm sick. I'm all alone." Her voice broke. "I'm so sick, Carol. Please come and help me. But don't tell anyone I called. Or where I am."

"Of course I'll come—"

"*Please.* Don't tell *anyone.*" Prilla burst into tears.

"I won't, Prilla. But what's the matter?"

She coughed, a deep, raspy sound. "Just come."

The line went dead.

Carol blinked, then replaced the handset. With a whoop, she clapped her hands and said to Pascal, "Prilla's alive!"

With his usual contempt for sudden movements, the cat ran for the bedroom.

She chuckled at his reaction, but puzzled at her own. Had she really felt that shaky about Prilla's well-being? After all, she'd been sighted twice.

Now Carol had confirmation that Prilla had returned to the Loch Mallaig area. Prilla must have used a cell phone to call from the lighthouse, but where had she gotten it? Maybe her wretched excuse for a father had accidentally forgotten the phone before leaving her alone and sick.

Her initial relief fading, Carol gritted her teeth and debated her next move. Should she call the chief? Harvey? Her partners?

But Prilla had pleaded that she tell no one. Carol could still hear the near hysteria in her voice. Her friend didn't need more chaos in her life right now.

Though she sat down and tried to calm herself so she could think clearly and decide what to do, Carol's mind raced in a million directions. It was obvious that her brain wouldn't quiet until she got up and did something.

How long had it been since Prilla had eaten? That might be part of her problem.

Carol grabbed a backpack from the closet and ransacked her kitchen cabinets. Before long, the pack held saltines, apple juice boxes, dried fruit, peanut butter crackers, and granola bars. It was doubtful that the lighthouse had power, but she tossed in a few cans of soup as well. She didn't know exactly what ailed Prilla, so Carol raided her medicine cabinet for over-the-counter remedies to ease a variety of maladies.

Though Carol planned to drive as close to the lighthouse as possible, she threw on hiking clothes and boots. Sunrise had passed but the morning sky hadn't brightened, so she added rain gear to the backpack.

At the door, the big decision confronted her once more: Should she call anyone before she left? If so, whom?

She couldn't call Harvey. Ruin his conference? No way.

Since the chief may not welcome unconfirmed information, she preferred not to call him until she actually connected with Prilla. That way, she could accurately describe her situation.

Her partners? Fresh alarm rose in Carol as she checked the antique clock on the mantel. Was she already late for work?

Whew. She'd only been asleep ten minutes or so when Prilla had called. Carol's stomach didn't calm, though, as her mental debate about whether to call Laura and Molly revived. They certainly didn't need Carol playing hooky today, but they'd ask all sorts of questions—and insist on accompanying her, which Prilla likely couldn't handle in her current state.

She tamped down her guilt, telling herself the morning's baking load was light and Laura and Molly could handle it easily without her. Carol texted that she had an urgent errand to run and would check in after it was done. Not exactly a lie, although it did prompt a series of responses asking for clarification and whether she was all right—all of which she ignored.

After hurrying through a few final tasks, Carol took her backpack to the Chrysler and set out for the lighthouse. She drove as far as she could, then parked her car at a dead end and shouldered the heavy knapsack.

The dark gray sky had lightened somewhat, but no early morning sun peeked through the clouds or dripping trees as Carol walked through the woods. The solemn little brook she crossed reawakened the small undercurrent of disquiet trickling through her. She'd managed to ignore it before her hike, but now she truly felt how alone she was.

Trying to ignore her doubt, Carol gritted her teeth and increased her speed, confident of her direction because she and her friends had hiked here recently.

Only this time, an empty lighthouse wouldn't await her. She hadn't helped Birdie, but this time, she'd find Prilla and take care of her.

Before she knew it, the lighthouse loomed before her like castle ruins in the mist. Bolstered by the increasing wind, Lake Superior's dark, gray-green waves lunged at the shoreline.

Carol paused. The forest's dankness had seeped into her bones, feeding her undercurrent of fear. From its dark depths, an image surfaced: the Celtic sign of death that had blackened her photo. A hundred shivers spiraled through her and froze her skin, until a familiar voice pierced the quiet air.

"Carol? Carol!" Prilla, white-faced and hunched, stood in the doorway of the small building attached to the lighthouse.

Carol wanted to drop to her knees for a prayer of thanksgiving. She wanted to yell at Prilla for standing out in the cold when she was unwell. Instead, she ran and gathered the quivering woman in a hug.

"Thank you for coming," Prilla murmured brokenly as she led Carol inside the building. "I'm sorry. I'm so sorry."

"It's all right." Carol rubbed her back. Prilla felt slightly feverish.

A throat cleared nearby.

Raising her head, Carol found herself staring down the barrel of a gun.

"Welcome to Nilson Castle, Carol," a deep voice said. "Care to come in and stay a while?"

14

Carol couldn't move. All she saw was the darkness of the gun's infinite barrel.

"I didn't want to call you," Prilla said hoarsely. "But Dad—he—" She broke down.

Prilla didn't have to say the words. Nilson had threatened her, probably held the gun to his daughter's head just as he was pointing it at Carol now.

"Prilla *does* have a cold," Nilson said. "So she didn't really lie."

As if you care about lying. Carol bit her tongue to keep from expressing her thoughts.

"And we are glad to see you, Carol," he went on, his voice unnervingly rich and warm. "Especially as I'm guessing you brought food. Prilla, take that backpack from your friend—move slowly, that's it. Now open it and put it on that chair."

Resistance wasn't a good option right now, so Carol let the bag slip from her shoulders.

At the sound of its zipper, Nilson grunted to Prilla, "Is her phone in there? Just hand it to me. Then open the backpack wide." He took the phone, then peered into the bag, his gun still trained on Carol. "Well, your friend must want us to live a long time. Food, aspirin, cough syrup—good. I won't have to listen to your hacking at night. Echoes in this place like you wouldn't believe."

Prilla said nothing. She just continued rummaging through the backpack while Nilson rifled alongside her.

"Food's too healthy for my taste," he commented, pulling out a can of vegetable soup, "but definitely better than nothing."

Carol finally dislodged her gaze from the gun and glanced around, assessing her dank surroundings. Pockmarked stucco walls were splotched with black mold, and the only illumination came from the weak daylight entering through cracks in the boarded windows. "I can heat up that soup for Prilla if you have a microwave or range." Not that she even saw a kitchen. "It might help her feel better."

"Well, aren't you the sweetheart?" A mocking smile stretched across Nilson's grizzled face. "No, we don't have such luxuries in this castle. Don't even have electricity, but thanks all the same."

"Prilla could eat it cold—"

"You let me worry about Prilla, okay?" Nilson barked. "You probably should worry more about yourself."

Carol fell quiet, silenced by his menacing smirk.

He motioned with the gun, revealing a glimpse of body armor covering his chest. "Now Prilla, we're going to take your friend to her own special spot down in the cellar. And don't forget, I'll be right behind you."

"The cellar?" His daughter's eyes widened. "But you told me—"

"Changing one's mind isn't just a woman's prerogative." His smile thinned. "It's certainly a father's. Especially for a troublemaker."

"Carol's not a troublemaker." Prilla's eyes sparkled. "She's my friend."

Nilson appeared almost as surprised as Carol felt, but Prilla's defiance lost its force when a coughing fit seized her.

Nilson's eyes hardened. "This woman's been nothing but trouble. Stalking us. Poking her nose into our business. Not what I consider friendship." He gestured with the gun again. "Now do what I say, or you might join her. It won't be a fun party."

Prilla cringed, her spark turned to ash.

"You'll both be in the Michigan basement." He flashed a wicked grin at Carol. "You're a newcomer to the UP, aren't you? Do you know what that is?"

"Yes." Carol bit off the word, trying not to imagine a century-old crawl space with a dirt floor and walls that wept with swampy condensation.

"You can take comfort in the fact you probably won't be alone," Nilson continued. "When it's cold, lots of wildlife come to visit."

Carol closed her eyes, unable to bear his face. Or the prospect of a muddy hole in the ground, a refuge for anything that hadn't yet hibernated.

Prilla touched Carol's shoulder, a reminder that resisting Nilson was futile. At least for now.

He pulled a small flashlight from his pocket and handed it to Prilla. She switched on the beam, then led Carol through a scarred door and down a narrow set of creaking stairs while Nilson followed. With each step, the temperature dropped. The musty air stank of rot, and Prilla coughed again.

As they reached the bottom, Carol fought her growing despair. *Don't give in. That's what he wants.* "I've visited better castles," she said.

"Shut up," he snarled from behind her. "Prilla, open that door."

Prilla did as ordered and shined her flashlight into a cramped, empty closet that probably hadn't been dusted since 1920. Although plenty of spiderwebs covered the ceiling and wall, it wasn't as bad as Carol had expected. Still not a place she'd like to be locked into, of course.

The gun prodded Carol's back. "Move."

Carol obeyed.

The heavy door slammed shut, and Carol found herself in total darkness. A key turned in the lock as she sank to the ground. Her fingers explored a cracked, cement floor. At least it wasn't a genuine dirt-floored Michigan basement.

Carol listened. No scurrying of little clawed feet. No slithering.

She never thought she'd be thankful to be locked in a closet, but compared to the alternatives, perhaps this wasn't the worst.

Carol cradled her head in her hands, abhorred by her circumstances. It appeared she'd have plenty of time to ponder ways to escape this mess—though right now, a getaway seemed as likely as taking a trip to the moon.

Even if she somehow gained her freedom, what would she say to Harvey? That sweet man had worried about leaving, yet trusted her to make wise decisions and take care of herself.

If she got out of this, he might insist on driving her to work every day.

If he didn't, Jenny would. Carol's head sank lower. Despite her determination not to cry, a tear ran down her cheek. After this fiasco, would her caring, conscientious daughter trust her to keep the grandchildren overnight? Take them on trips?

And her friends—after Prilla's phone call, she should have told Laura and Molly, brainstormed with them about solutions, and allowed them to help. That was what friends did for each other.

As for Prilla, keeping a troubled person's confidence wasn't always the wise thing to do. That approach certainly hadn't helped Prilla or herself.

Carol groaned. If only she hadn't forced herself to learn these lessons the hard way.

Too upset to formulate any sort of escape plan, Carol gripped her hands and prayed.

She'd sat in the dark closet for what felt like days, but Carol figured it wasn't yet past noon. She wasn't hungry, though she wished fervently for her water bottle.

She hadn't heard any noise from upstairs, but an odd rumbling had caught her ear once or twice. At first Carol thought it was thunder, but it wasn't quite the same. She wished she could put her finger on the sound.

Had Nilson allowed Prilla to eat something? If not, he was obviously quite unconcerned with his daughter's well-being. Was it merely selfish disregard for her health, or was he mistreating her in more violent ways? If he was responsible for Kristen's murder—and at the moment, that seemed quite likely—he clearly had little concern for his children's lives.

Carol knew she couldn't focus on that worry. It solved nothing and only served to darken her already bleak mood.

While pondering Nilson's reasons for luring her here didn't brighten her situation, it did compel her mind to focus. Determining his motivation might help her communicate with him, the first step to getting her and Prilla out of here.

Nilson was articulate and smart enough to have evaded the police for the months since his insurance fraud had come to light. It wasn't hard to picture him carefully groomed, wearing an expensive suit, using that smile and voice to talk people out of their life savings.

So why had he brought Carol here? He should be leaving the country, not weighing himself down with another hostage, one who didn't possess much money or any particularly helpful means of escape.

Tired of trying to puzzle out Nilson's warped brain—and not daring to think how he could use her very life as a bargaining tool—she wondered how soon anyone would notice something was wrong.

Would her partners, left out of the loop, take Carol's pursuing a lead without them in stride? Or would they find it troubling? Would they check in with Chief Thomson or Harvey?

Carol frowned. More likely, Laura and Molly would be miffed

because she'd ducked out of work without a good explanation. They might give her a chance, though, even wait an entire day before calling her out for not responding to their texts.

For a moment, she lost herself in a vision of Bread on Arrival's warm, cheerful kitchen, full of light and laughter and wonderful smells. She mentally strode to the front of the house, where antique display counters were laden with row after row of beautiful pastries, and customers chatted with each other and the bakehouse staff. Carol would give anything to be cleaning off tables and hauling bus pans instead of stuck in a dark basement far from civilization.

She tried not to think of Harvey, but it was no use. She knew he might have called her cell phone, but the first day at a conference was always hectic, and he often worked well into the night. This morning—was it only this morning he'd left?—she'd been groggy and grouchy. If only she'd savored his embrace a moment longer . . .

Jenny rarely called during Carol's workday since she taught all day, and her evenings were full of the hustle-bustle of family life with young kids.

Deer hunters might find Carol's car, parked at that dead end in the middle of nowhere, but they'd simply assume she was one of them. It might sit there for weeks.

From what Carol could surmise, only Pascal and the chickens would notice her absence today, and they'd be plenty put out. Eventually, everyone else would join in their frustration. Their reproaches, however, couldn't begin to match Carol's. She'd been naïve. Careless. *Stupid, stupid, stupid!*

Carol ranted at herself until she realized that too was counterproductive. Yes, she should have wondered if Nilson was bullying Prilla into lying, but her friend's clearly failing health had grabbed her attention first and foremost.

As Harvey reminded her, acting from her heart rather than her head had gotten her in trouble more than once. Carol furrowed her brow. If she had to make mistakes, she'd rather overdo kindness than underdo it.

That affirmed, she shifted her attention to forming an escape plan. What could a fifty-something woman, locked in a closet without even a flashlight, let alone a weapon, do to escape a career criminal with a gun?

First, she might check to see if this holding cell was as solid as it appeared. Perhaps a rotten board or two might present an escape opportunity. But could Carol stand the thought of probing the dusty, cobwebby walls with bare fingers?

She located tissues in her jeans pocket and used them to shield her fingers as she blindly poked and prodded the wall. They provided little real protection from spiders, but the psychological barrier was helpful enough.

As far as she could tell, the closet contained no weak, rotten spots she might exploit. It was completely empty, containing not even an old shoe she could use as a weapon. She rattled the doorknob, but neither the iron hardware nor the thick wood door budged. Nilson had chosen her prison well.

She could scream herself hoarse, but even if her voice carried outside, the lighthouse's remote location ensured no passerby would hear her. Nilson, however, would certainly hear her and wouldn't take kindly to her efforts.

Weary, covered with cobwebs, and coming up empty-handed in terms of escape plans, Carol sat again, debating whether she dared lie down.

The odd rumble sounded again. She perked up her ears, detecting what sounded like patterns of speech. Was it a movie or something Nilson was watching upstairs? No, that wasn't right. The building had no electricity.

A new sound erupted. *Pop-pop-pop-pop-pop!*

Fireworks?

Carol's breath solidified in her chest. That wasn't fireworks. It was gunshots.

15

Carol had flattened herself on the floor for untold minutes, remaining there even after the barrage ceased. Although she did Pilates on a regular basis, every joint in her body rebelled against the dank, cement floor.

Still she lay, listening and trembling. What was going on outside the closet? Carol weighed the possibilities. If Nilson had decided to get rid of Prilla, he could have done so with a single shot. But why kill Prilla first? Why was Carol still alive?

She hated trying to think like a criminal, but she wouldn't survive long if she didn't attempt to understand his logic.

A tiny flow of hope coursed through her. Had someone attempted a rescue? Even as she tried to calm her expectations, bubbles of joy and nausea mingled in her stomach.

When a key turned in the lock, her queasy insides suffered another lurch. Nevertheless, if Nilson was coming for her, she wouldn't let him find her cowering on the floor. A moment after Carol sat up, the flashlight shone in her eyes.

"I'm sorry, Carol." Prilla's voice trembled, and she shifted the beam down.

Nilson's tall shadow—including the silhouette of his gun—hovered behind his daughter. "Get up and come out."

Whatever he had in mind, Carol couldn't wait to leave this stinking basement behind.

"Up the stairs," he ordered.

When they reached the main floor, Carol blinked. Even gray light filtering through the dirty window shocked her eyes, but she still drank it in.

"On your knees," Nilson snapped. Folding his long frame into a military crouch that was impressively agile for someone his age, he somehow managed to keep the gun aimed at them as he hustled to a door at one end of the room.

Nilson had moved with a panther's deadly grace, despite carrying a heavy-looking backpack on his shoulder and holding a different, larger gun. What little knowledge Carol possessed about firearms she'd learned from her dad's hunting. This gun appeared to be a semiautomatic rifle with a scope. Why the change?

"Stay down and move past the window," Nilson hissed. "Get over here. Hurry."

As she and Prilla scuttled across the splintery floor like spooked crabs, Carol recalled the earlier gunshots and wondered if Nilson had fired them from his gun. The walls were rutted, but with age, not fresh bullet holes, so he must have shot at someone outside. But who?

She pushed forward on all fours, knees complaining as she scurried toward the door Nilson had indicated. Nilson ordered Prilla to open the door, which led to another stairway—this one spiraling up toward what used to be the beacon. What treads there were appeared made of iron, but occasional gaps occurred in the rusty, old steps. Could the staircase hold her weight, let alone that of two other adults?

"Both of you, climb," Nilson commanded. "And don't stop until you reach the top." He prodded Carol with the gun. "You first."

With no choice, Carol started to ascend the steps.

She couldn't help glancing back at Prilla. Wheezing and coughing, the younger woman was struggling before they reached the third step.

If only the stairway weren't so narrow, she could have taken Prilla's arm and helped her.

"Do you have to be such a pain?" Nilson asked his daughter through bared teeth.

"She's doing the best she can," Carol snapped.

With lightning speed, Nilson lunged past Prilla and slapped Carol across the face.

Cheek stinging, she grabbed the shaky rail. The spiral staircase below wavered—

"Anything else to say about how I treat my own kid?" Nilson growled.

She had plenty more to say, but decided to keep it to herself.

Prilla had stuffed her fist in her mouth, her eyes desperately apologetic, but Nilson didn't seem to notice as he returned to the step below hers. "Now move," he said. "Both of you."

Carol continued the climb up the spiral, praying Prilla wouldn't stumble and fall. Sometimes the stairway rattled and swayed, but Carol gripped the railing.

By the time they reached the top, Prilla was gasping for air and nearly crawling.

The staircase opened into a small room with disintegrating plaster walls. Large windows lined its sides. The lighthouse's illumination mechanism had been removed. Perhaps the state had taken it for a museum display.

"Sit!" Nilson barked.

Carol helped Prilla to the ground, then squeezed her hand. The woman leaned against her, breath ragged.

She probably needed antibiotics and an inhaler, but Carol knew better than to suggest her seeing a doctor. They had more pressing issues at the moment anyway, like the armed madman holding them captive.

Carol gazed around the lantern room, more thankful than ever to see sky. She wished she could see the vast panorama of Lake Superior, but she could hear waves slapping at the rocks below.

The rocks below . . . Carol recalled the awful account of the high school boy who had lost his life there. She caught her breath. Had Nilson brought them up here to push them off?

But why exert such effort, when killing her and Prilla could have been so much simpler? He had more than one gun, after all.

Shoving the thoughts aside, Carol turned away from the window and focused on comforting Prilla, but she was soon distracted by Nilson's next move.

He army-crawled to a door on one side of the room and threw it open. Chilly air rushed in. Flashing his wicked smile, Nilson called to Carol, "Are you afraid of heights?"

Her answer wouldn't matter, she knew, but she raised her chin. "No."

"Great." Before she knew it, he'd slid beside her. Poking the gun in her side, he said in his golden tone, "Now, Prilla, I want you to sit still while Carol and I go for a little walk. If you move or cause trouble, I'll shoot her or push her off the lighthouse. Understand?"

Cowering against the wall, Prilla nodded.

With another jab of the gun barrel, he ordered Carol, "Crawl to the door."

Once again, she obeyed, seeing no other option that wouldn't endanger herself or Prilla.

"Stand up," he said when they reached the doorway.

"No!" Prilla cried.

He rounded on his daughter. "Another word out of you, and you'll follow her."

Slowly, Carol rose from her crouch. Wind and rain assaulted her face. She clung to the wet, slippery doorframe with both hands and gasped.

Below was a horseshoe of police vehicles, lights flashing like red and blue flames. Hope surged through Carol at the idea of being rescued.

Though the tempest nearly blew her off her feet, a thrill of gladness lifted Carol's heart into the clouds. The joy soared even higher when she identified Chief Thomson's familiar voice rumbling through a bullhorn. That's what she'd heard when she'd been shut up in the closet.

As Nilson hunkered behind her, however, the chief began bargaining with her captor—but with apparently little leverage.

"We can talk about your requests, Nilson," the chief said. "But first, you must release Carol and Prilla."

Nilson laughed as if sharing a joke at a party, then projected his golden stage voice. "That would make it nice and convenient for your SWAT team, wouldn't it? No, I'm afraid that's not acceptable."

The man didn't need a bullhorn. Clutching the doorframe even more tightly, Carol leaned forward to hear Thomson's reply.

None yet. No doubt he was weighing his options.

Clinging to the rain-slick doorframe, Carol was reminded of the view from a Ferris wheel. She stared at clumps of miniature people scattered among cars, ambulances, fire trucks, and news vans against a backdrop of dark evergreens and glorious fall foliage. Uniformed officers were everywhere, but she saw civilians too. A bright red spot grabbed her eye.

Harvey's rain slicker?

She tried to swallow the tears that poured into her throat. No, she couldn't collapse now. She had to bear up, not only for herself, but for Harvey. For Jenny and her family. For her friends. For Prilla—

Stay strong. The words seemed to be etched across the menacing sky. *Stay strong,* she repeated to herself, engraving the phrase into her heart.

Not sure what else to do, she clung to her spot in the doorway, waiting for whatever would happen next. When Nilson spoke again,

Carol momentarily lost her grip and almost slipped onto the rickety catwalk that encircled the lantern room.

Barely catching herself, she shook as her captor put forth his requests. He reminded Carol of a telemarketer selling time-shares. "The ladies and I would like a boat, because we want to take a trip," he called to the chief. "Not a junky little fishing boat, but something appropriate for their needs and comfort. One that can handle the lake well. Since I can't currently access my own personal funds, we'll also need money—say, at least a hundred thousand in cash, unmarked, of course, and in a briefcase. We are in a bit of a hurry." Nilson sounded almost apologetic. "Might we expect your cooperation by four o'clock this afternoon?"

"We will consider your request," Thomson said, his tone firm.

Carol felt the rifle's barrel in her back again.

"Please consider this a most urgent petition," Nilson called to the chief. Lowering his voice, he hissed at Carol, "Move forward. Onto the catwalk."

Her stomach lurched at the thought.

"Don't worry." Nilson jabbed her again. "I'll be right behind you."

Taking a deep breath, Carol reminded herself to stay strong. She straightened her shoulders and stepped out onto the catwalk.

Its shivering matched hers. She grabbed the rail, but it was so wobbly she let go immediately.

"Move closer to the other side," Nilson snarled. "Now."

If she took baby steps, keeping her eyes on her feet, she could do this. Step. Step. Carol reached a tentative hand toward the rail on the opposite side, which was thankfully more stable than the other. Step.

She didn't hear Nilson follow or feel the catwalk shake with his weight, but she didn't need to feel the gun's barrel to know it was pointed straight at her.

The chief's bullhorn boomed again. "Please let Carol return to the lighthouse, and we'll do our best to fulfill your request."

"Your best had better be exactly what I want." Nilson's golden tone had tarnished.

"We'll do everything we can," Chief Thomson repeated.

The wind shifted direction and whipped Carol's hair into her eyes, obscuring her vision. *Just as well.* She didn't think she could stand seeing the bright red spot on the ground any longer.

When Nilson finally ordered her back, Carol's frozen body and brain couldn't comply. She clung to the railing.

"What, you like it out there?" he jeered.

Facing outward, she couldn't see his horrible grin, but she heard it. Fortunately, the anger it generated melted the iciness in her mind and limbs. Slowly, Carol turned and stepped back toward the lantern room.

"Good job," Nilson said as they went inside the slightly warmer room. "After that, we should have what we need in no time. Maybe even before four."

Prilla was huddled against a wall, but her face showed relief when Carol returned safely.

Safe? Ha. Carol knew she and Prilla were anything but—especially when she watched with horror as Nilson removed a bundle of rope from his backpack and eyed the women with a menacing glint in his eye.

He stepped closer, uncoiling the rope. "Time to get comfortable, ladies."

16

If only the SWAT team could rescue them through the crack in the lighthouse wall where Nilson kept vigil with a pair of binoculars. He had swapped out his larger gun for the smaller one again, and although he didn't keep it trained on the bound women sitting against the wall, the threat remained.

Prilla had dozed off, her clammy, feverish forehead resting on Carol's shoulder. Still awake, Carol was forced to listen to Nilson's self-congratulatory monologue.

"Well, if it isn't the Coast Guard, towing our boat out in the lake," he crowed. "Looks like a good one. Not great, but pretty good."

Instead of responding to Nilson, Carol peeked down at Prilla. The sick woman was getting some rest, thank goodness. Carol watched as the taut lines in her friend's pale face softened. If only her reprieve wasn't doomed to be temporary.

"Looks like they don't know quite what to do," Nilson continued. "I'd better help them out."

Carol expected him to start calling out instructions. She didn't expect him to stuff the rifle's barrel into the wall slit and let loose a round of fire that shook the room.

Prilla awoke with a scream.

As the shots continued, Carol realized she was screaming too. Moving awkwardly with her bound limbs, she flung herself against Prilla so they both lay flat on the floor. When the horrifying sound of gunfire ceased, she lifted her head and strained to see what was happening. Why had Nilson stopped firing? He hadn't dropped to the floor, so he must be unharmed.

Nilson opened the door to the catwalk, and Carol stiffened. Would he make her go out there again?

But he didn't glance her way. "Just wanted you to know I'm watching," he called down to Chief Thomson, his tone almost sickeningly friendly. "No need to fire back."

"I'd rather not fire on a building with two hostages inside, but I need you to not endanger my men. We're doing all we can for you," the chief replied through his bullhorn.

"We don't have to make this hostile," Nilson said. "Just listen to a few instructions, give me what I want, then leave. Bring the boat to the lighthouse dock and tie it up. Put the money in a briefcase and leave it in front of the dock. Put the keys to the boat just inside the boathouse, on the shelf to the left of the door. Then I want the Coast Guard gone. *Gone,* as in miles away. Any attempt to follow us—boat, helicopter, whatever—you know what will happen."

Chief Thomson's response was sharp, indicating he was tiring of Nilson's attitude. "If you harm anyone—be it a hostage or any officer of the law or the Coast Guard—we will open fire, and you will not survive. Do you understand?"

Nilson didn't reply, but he hovered near the slit for a while, taking random peeks before ducking to the floor. Prilla turned on her side and curled up to Carol, who welcomed the warmth to her stiffening joints. She must have fallen asleep too, dozing until Nilson began talking again.

He held up his watch. "Only half an hour until four o'clock. Think they'll meet my requests before deadline?" He aimed a teasing look at the door to the catwalk.

"What are you talking about?" Prilla whimpered.

"Well, if they're not reasonable, who knows what may happen?"

"Don't listen to him," Carol whispered in her friend's ear. "Turn your face away." Hardening her expression, Carol followed her own advice.

Prilla shook with stifled sobs, but she kept quiet as her father continued the countdown to four o'clock. With each passing minute his demands didn't appear to be met, a grating note in his voice grew. Would his temper detonate before the deadline?

Just when Carol feared he'd explode, Nilson chuckled, though the sound wasn't much more comforting than his irritation. "How about that? They've brought the boat to the dock. And what do you know? I do believe that's the police chief who's laying the briefcase by the dock."

Carol choked, suddenly filled with terror that the chief was a sitting duck.

Nilson laughed, clearly reading her thoughts. "Think, Carol. Not that I love your police chief, but killing him would be counterproductive with all these cops around. I'd like to live to spend that money." He struck a righteous pose. "Never kill, except out of true necessity. That's my motto."

Carol furrowed her brow. Had he considered Kristen's death a true necessity? Would he view killing Carol and Prilla the same way?

Carol turned away again, not wanting to spend too long contemplating the answers.

Nilson checked the slit again and began to whistle. "Well, ladies. As luxurious as this castle is, it is time to leave it." He untied Prilla, then made her untie Carol while he put his backpack on. "Stand up. We'll go downstairs again, as we did before. Prilla, then Carol, with yours truly bringing up the rear."

His jovial mood faded when they arrived downstairs and he peered through a window. The storm had grown worse. Still pointing the gun at the women, he pulled a heavy rain poncho out of his backpack.

"Where's Prilla's?" Carol asked as she watched him put it on.

Nilson snorted, and Carol steamed with disgust. He clearly hadn't allowed Prilla to pack anything before he dragged her here. And now he expected poor, sick Prilla to trudge through this weather to the boat. Carol hazarded a glance at Prilla, expecting that spark she'd seen before. Instead, her friend stared at her feet, limp hands hanging at her side.

Don't give up, Prilla.

"Prilla can wear my poncho." Carol took a calculated risk in striding a few steps to where Nilson had discarded her backpack earlier. There were worse things to be shot for than trying to offer a small comfort to a sick friend.

Instead of firing his gun, Nilson smirked as Carol withdrew her poncho. "How nice of you."

Carol ignored him and handed the plastic garment to Prilla.

"Thank you, Carol," Prilla whispered as she put it on.

"Before we head for the boat, let's do a little review together," Nilson said. "Listen closely, and do exactly what I say." His tone had sharpened, and his eyes glittered. Nilson motioned to Carol with the rifle. "You will stand beside Prilla. In a minute, we're going to walk together. Both of you, keep the pace steady. I'll hold this rifle nice and high so all your cop friends out there can see I mean business." His smile morphed into a snarl. "Don't even think of trying something, or you'll both die."

Though Nilson had repeated similar warnings earlier, Carol reminded herself not to underestimate his intentions. Cornered, yet close to freedom, he wouldn't let anything or anyone stand in his way.

She devised her own plan to create little distractions that would change the rhythm of Nilson's scheme. Disturbing his concentration for even a few seconds might prove enough for the SWAT team to intervene.

Hoping to somehow draw Prilla in as an accomplice, she glanced toward her friend. Prilla was staring into space, her face pale and drawn, her eyes sunken.

Nilson interrupted Carol's thoughts. "We'll stop just before we reach that briefcase Chief Thomson left for me by the dock. Carol, you'll pick it up and hold it to your side until I say otherwise. Now open the door, Prilla. Let's go."

Prilla did as commanded, and they went out into the storm. The wind howled at them, and the rain fell in sheets. Soaked within seconds, Carol tucked her head against the tempest. She sensed a hundred eyes on them and wished it made her feel safer.

As they headed toward the dock, Carol knew Harvey's gaze was locked on her. If only she could push aside these curtains of rain and look into her husband's eyes. Where was the red raincoat?

When she didn't see it, she knew where he was. Chief Thomson had insisted Harvey stay toward the rear, where he wouldn't be tempted to do anything foolish. At least the rain camouflaged the tears that flowed down her cheeks. Her grief doubled when she realized Harvey would be stuck explaining all this to Jenny, to Mimi, to Molly and Laura, to all her loved ones. How could she leave him to that grim duty?

They fought the wind with every step. Even if she managed to distract Nilson, would this weather make it impossible for the SWAT team to rescue them?

Carol forced herself to focus on the briefcase. It looked solid enough—perhaps it would work as a weapon. First, though, she'd have to create an opportunity to swing it at him. But how?

As they trudged along, Prilla slowed so that Carol nearly bumped into her. On the next stride, Prilla's warm pinkie brushed Carol's fingers as if to indicate she was glad she wasn't alone.

The tiny gesture poured strength into Carol, and she refocused on devising a plan. A moment later, she intentionally kicked a stone, hoping the noise might startle Nilson into pointing his rifle in the rock's direction and away from Prilla. But the stormy wind and lake devoured the sound. Nilson didn't even flinch.

"Could we go a little slower?" Carol ventured. "The cold's giving me a cramp in my side."

"Poor thing," Nilson jeered, then reached ahead to prod Prilla as if she were the one who had disrupted his schedule. "Both of you, get a move on."

Carol hunched, hoping she was convincing. "If you want me to keep walking, we need to stop a second."

He swore vividly, but halted. Like lightning, he transferred the rifle's barrel from Prilla to Carol's temple. Her heartbeat shot into overdrive.

"Think you can walk now?" he snarled.

Slowly, with the cold metal pressed to her head, Carol straightened. As they walked, she made her imaginary cramp disappear. No chance for the SWAT team on this try.

Carol cast sideways glances at her fellow hostage, hoping to catch her eye. She had to communicate her intentions somehow. But the woman kept her focus on the ground as she walked. Tears gushed down her cheeks, as if Nilson's threat to Carol was the last straw.

When they reached the briefcase, Nilson ground the gun barrel into Carol's temple again. "Stop. Carol, pick up the briefcase. Hold it close to your body. I don't want you to get any ideas about smacking me with it."

Fuming that he had guessed her plan, she slowly grasped the handle and drew it to her side. A hundred thousand dollars weighed more than she'd expected.

Nilson's other arm snaked along her back, and his big, clammy hand closed over hers, setting off a wave of queasiness in her. Still keeping the gun at her head, he took the briefcase. "Good job. Now, let's head for the boat. Remember, if either of you try anything funny, you'll regret it."

They continued onto the wooden dock. The lake's waves now crashed against the boathouse and flooded the dock, making it hard for them to keep their feet. The boat brought by the Coast Guard rose and fell as if it were a fishing bobber.

Nilson had them halt again at the boathouse. "Carol, push the door open. It should be unlocked. Reach inside and grab the keys."

The battered door groaned open, and Carol's hand closed around the keys. She longed to throw the keys out to sea and watch them disappear into the waves.

"Do it, and you'll follow them," Nilson growled.

Without looking at him, Carol handed over the keys. He poked her with the gun again, and she and Prilla resumed their sad, slippery route to the boat.

Suddenly, Prilla halted in her tracks.

"What's the matter with you? Walk." Nilson shifted the aim of his gun to Prilla's head.

"Dad?" Prilla's voice was soft, but she repeated it louder. "Dad, you know I'm afraid of the lake."

"It's just water. Walk," he commanded hoarsely.

"I-I can't. I'm afraid."

"Don't be stupid. Do as I say."

Prilla didn't budge. "You helped me on the beach that day, remember?"

Carol envisioned a scared little girl in a ruffled bathing suit, tears erased by her father's strong arms around her.

"Shut up. Just shut up." Nilson's voice rose to a scream. "Walk! Or I'll shoot you right here."

The same moment Prilla fell to her knees, Carol felt the gun at the back of her head again.

"Get up!" Nilson dropped the briefcase. He dragged Prilla to her feet and shoved her forward. "Pick up the briefcase, Carol, and move. Both of you!"

After obeying, Prilla and Carol resumed their walk on the flooded dock, but Carol managed to brush her fingers against Prilla's. However, her caring gesture didn't seem to reassure Prilla, who was sobbing.

Nilson only grew angrier until Carol feared they wouldn't reach the boat alive.

"Hush, Prilla." Carol spoke sternly and gently. "Forget the lake. Remember the locket. Remember your mom."

The reminder didn't stop the cries, but Prilla's outburst waned.

Nilson's madness diminished as his daughter calmed, at least to the point Carol could breathe again. He took the briefcase. They edged along the dock, hungry waves licking their feet. Pinprick spray jabbed Carol's face. She gritted her teeth to control the shivering.

Once they boarded the boat and left, could the SWAT team help them anymore? Their chances of survival would plunge.

Like her freezing fingers, Carol's brain had numbed, but she forced it into action. Should she try to trip Nilson? Even if he didn't shoot her, the gun could go off, and she wasn't sure she was willing to risk that.

The boat now thrashed in the water beside them. A huge wave rolled over the end of the dock, soaking them all again.

Prilla screamed and recoiled.

"Shut up, I said!" Nilson roared, making a show of grasping Carol's arm roughly and grinding the gun into her temple.

Prilla covered her mouth with both hands.

Nilson pulled Carol close and growled into her ear, "You've been downright handy. Couldn't have made it this far without you."

Handy? Sickened, Carol realized why Nilson had lured her to the lighthouse. Prilla, near emotional collapse after days of illness and intimidation, was currently unpredictable. He couldn't depend on her, even at gunpoint, to remain still while he performed small but essential tasks like retrieving the briefcase and keys, distractions that might have opened him to the SWAT team's action.

At Prilla's worst moments, she might not care enough about her own life to perform the tasks either. But she couldn't bear the threat of his killing her friend. Neither, of course, could Carol. Nilson had played them off each other. With two lives on the line, he'd blackmailed the police into paralysis.

"Don't get the wrong idea, though," Nilson went on, his hot breath like acid on Carol's skin. "If you'd been as big a pain as Prilla, I'd have blown you away long before this."

It seemed an eternity before Nilson drew back and repositioned the gun to his daughter's head. He motioned Carol to step inside the boat, then pointed to the bow. "Stand over there."

While Carol was used to water, she clung to the side of the heaving boat, her stomach lurching with its bronco moves.

"Not there!" he bellowed when she paused. "In the front, where the boat's chained to the dock."

She staggered to the spot he indicated, then Nilson herded Prilla into the boat and pushed her down on a bench seat near Carol.

Struggling to keep his balance, he stretched and handed Carol the keys. "The small one probably unlocks the chain," he yelled above the storm. "Do that, and pull the chain into the boat. Then give the keys back."

The keys burned with possibility in Carol's cold hands. *If only* . . . But Nilson held the trump card—his daughter's life.

Carol found the key and unlocked the heavy chain. With a heavy *clank*, it fell to the boat's deck. Turning to return the keys to Nilson, her gaze locked on to Prilla's.

Prilla's focus shifted to the chain lying at Carol's feet.

With effort, Carol didn't look down—or celebrate that Prilla had connected with her, maybe even hatched a plan. She threw the keys back to Nilson.

"Does this boat have a bathroom?" Prilla whined. "I feel sick."

He spat. "Not my problem."

Prilla burst into shrieking wails and collapsed at his feet, inches from where Carol had dropped the chain.

Nilson struggled to maintain his footing against the storm's fury and keep the gun trained on his daughter. In the moment he lost focus, Prilla grabbed the chain and slammed it at his knees.

He roared and dropped the gun, and Carol dove for it.

Nilson slipped and hit his head against the railing, then slumped motionless to the deck.

Carol grabbed the gun and aimed it at him.

But she kept her finger away from the trigger. No more bullets needed to be fired that day.

17

Shaking, Carol kept the gun trained at Nilson's head. She had no plans to shoot him, of course, but she wasn't going to take a single risk. He wouldn't hurt Prilla or her again.

"Carol, hand me the gun." Chief Thomson's gentle voice sounded in her ear, and his warm hand landed on her shoulder, making her jump. His men swarmed the heaving boat around them.

"I can't let go." Carol swallowed. Her fingers felt locked into place around the ugly weapon. "And the safety's not on."

Deftly, the chief clicked the safety into place and carefully dislodged her fingers from the handle. "It's okay. I have it."

"Carol! Carol, are you all right?" Harvey vaulted over the side of the boat. He swept Carol into his arms and held on for what felt like an eternity. She was crushed against him so hard that she could barely breathe, but at the moment she didn't care. After coming so close to being separated from him forever, what were a few bruised ribs?

Eventually, the enormity of what she'd done almost smothered Carol's joy at being reunited with him. "Harvey, I'm sorry. I'm so sorry. I was thinking with my heart instead of my head again."

"It's all right, honey. It's all right." He tightened his grip. "You helped rescue Prilla."

Although Carol continued to cling to her husband, she shifted her gaze to where Prilla was still huddled on the boat's deck. Chief Thomson was crouched beside her, coaxing her to come with him. When EMTs swarmed into the boat to treat and transport her wounded father to a hospital, she remained frozen.

Giving Harvey a last squeeze, Carol whispered, "Harvey, I think I'm needed."

"All right, but I'm not going anywhere."

"Good."

She knelt beside Prilla and touched her shoulder. "Prilla, you need to come with me out of this rain."

Prilla gave no sign of hearing.

"The storm's still rising," Carol persisted, "and the waves are getting bigger every moment. We can't leave you here. Come to my house and sit by the fire. I'll warm a bap for you."

A tiny light flickered in Prilla's blank eyes. "With cinnamon butter?"

"All the cinnamon butter you want." Carol hugged her, then helped Prilla to her feet.

Quaking from head to toe, Prilla clutched Carol's elbow. Harvey took Prilla's other arm, and the trio slowly left the boat behind.

"How is she?" Though Laura was calling Carol from the bakehouse, she whispered as if she'd awaken Prilla.

Carol smiled. "Still asleep. Her fever broke, so she seems comfortable. Goodness knows how long it's been since she's really slept."

"You should go back to bed too," Laura insisted. "After an ordeal like that, you should sleep a week."

"Tempting, but no thanks. We promised the chief we'd come in as soon as possible, and I doubt he'd take kindly to me staying in bed all day. Hopefully I can come to work soon." Carol infused her voice with gratitude. "You girls have been wonderful. Neither Prilla nor I would have survived without your concern. Your prayers."

"You can make up for it by washing every pan I use until Christmas."

At the sound of Laura's usual moxie, Carol grinned. It was a first step in the return to normalcy.

Prilla, after waking late and devouring the full Scottish breakfast Harvey prepared, appeared as clearheaded as Carol had ever seen her. Though pale and weak, she even seemed eager to talk to Chief Thomson.

First, though, Prilla wrapped her arms around Carol and buried her head in Carol's shoulder. For a full minute, she said nothing. Then she whispered, "Thank you."

A thousand words tangled in Carol's throat, but none of them could say what she felt. She didn't know how long they clung to each other before Prilla turned to Harvey and thanked him as well. "Except for my mom, I've never had friends like you."

Carol started to reply that she'd never had a friend like Prilla either, but she stopped herself as a vision of Birdie flashed in her mind. Shoving it aside, she collected a towel and toiletries for Prilla to shower before they were due in town for their meeting with Chief Thomson.

Marveling at how the weather had cleared, Carol, Harvey, and Prilla drove together to police headquarters in the town hall. Carol feared Wilma Guthrie, the department's big-haired, gossipy receptionist, would pounce on Prilla in search of information to leak to Loch Mallaig's gossip chain.

But it was Saturday, and a young officer sat at the desk. "Chief Thomson's on the phone right now," he said after Carol stated their business. "He'll see you in a minute or two."

They didn't wait long. Chief Thomson came out a few moments later to welcome them into his office, where Harvey and Carol took seats on either side of Prilla in front of the chief's desk. Once Thomson was in his own chair facing them, he invited Prilla to tell her story in her own words.

Carol had feared Prilla would freeze in the chief's presence. Instead, her story, long repressed, poured out of her. Chief Thomson didn't pepper Prilla with questions. He simply listened and made occasional notes.

Even before Kristen had shown up at Prilla's cabin, Nilson dropped in to stay a while. When Prilla asked her father why he'd been gone twenty-five years, he'd answered that Lena had been after him, and he had to hide. "That mean woman" was still trying to get him in trouble with the police. Then he had some unpaid debts to people who just wouldn't wait for their money, and . . .

When Prilla blurted that because of his disappearance, she'd been accused of murdering Boersma, he'd told her he was sorry. He wanted to make it up to her. He wanted them to be a family.

Harvey's fingers gripped the arms of his chair. Carol barely kept from unleashing her very unkind thoughts on the situation.

"He sounded different from the other times I'd seen him," Prilla explained. "I thought he really meant it." Her face held such heartbreak that Carol longed to stop the interview and hug all the hurt out of her. "I should have realized that he was on the run again, because he was so secretive." She looked to Carol. "That's why I didn't come to the bakery as much, why I didn't talk to you that night at the grocery store. He didn't want me to talk to anybody."

Prilla went on to reveal that a few days later, Kristen had also shown up, intending to stay for an extended time. Kristen hadn't been happy to see her father, and the feeling was definitely mutual. They both made a constant mess of the cabin and they fought nearly constantly, until Kristen started to bug Nilson for money.

"She said she'd tell the police about him if he didn't give her five thousand dollars. I'd given both of them all I could, but she was never happy." Prilla's head drooped. "The night she died, she was at her worst. Apparently she'd gotten bored of being at the cabin and was looking for some fun at my expense." Prilla shuddered and went silent.

Carol rubbed her friend's back. "It's okay, just tell us when you're ready."

"I will." Prilla changed the subject. "Matt had a bad reputation for being a womanizer, but he was nicer to me than anybody. He was impressed by my art, and he even introduced me to his parents. I was devastated when he was killed, and I've always put flowers at Faerie Copse on the anniversary of his death. Kristen knew that I'd be there that night, so she decided to play a Month of the Faeries prank on me." Prilla grimaced, then collected herself. "She drew that Celtic symbol on her face, then lay on the ground and arranged a knife so it looked like it was sticking out of her chest. When I found her, I nearly died of fright."

"My goodness," Carol murmured, unable to think of anything else to say.

"Kristen drew the symbol on herself?" Chief Thomson's brow furrowed.

"Yes," Prilla confirmed. "We had words, of course. She told me I was simple and weak, and that I let our father push me around. But she boasted that he was about to get his comeuppance courtesy of Mr. Bryan Strong, and that she was going to be there to watch. Eventually I'd had enough, and I stormed off and left her in the copse."

"What happened next?" the chief asked.

"Later that evening, my father returned from being gone. I didn't know where. He changed his clothes as soon as he got back, then he was impatient to leave. That's when he made me go with him to the lighthouse."

"How did he know about the lighthouse?" Carol asked. "It seems as if most people in this area would rather forget about it."

A faint flush stained Prilla's pale cheeks. "He told me that when he was a boy, my grandfather used to take him there sometimes. Grandpa liked that everybody thought it was haunted. That made it a good place to hide stuff he'd stolen."

Crime clearly runs in this family. Carol shook her head. How had Prilla escaped its influence? Maybe her mom had made the difference.

"The lighthouse was so creepy." Prilla shuddered. "I didn't want to leave my home, my art. I've always been afraid of water too, especially during storms. But then I hated staying inside, day after day, because I've always hiked in the forest. I missed the trees, the birds, and the animals. He only let me come to town sometimes to buy groceries." Her cheeks pinked again, and she pulled her gaze from the chief to a spot behind him. "Once, he told me to go to the library and sneak out a clipping from their newspaper archives." She slowly returned her gaze to Carol. "One from when you and your partners opened the bakery."

Carol inhaled sharply. The photo he'd sullied with the Celtic death symbol.

"He said he wanted me to have the picture, since you and I were friends, but that made no sense. And once I brought it to the lighthouse, it disappeared." Prilla wrung her hands. "I never wanted to steal anything. I hate stealing."

"If the library needs a new copy, I'm sure the newspaper will provide it," Thomson said kindly.

Carol patted Prilla's hand. "Don't worry about it."

Reassured, Prilla told them that though she'd kept it secret from Nilson, she had stopped by Blanche's, bringing her what food she could spare, much to the older woman's delight. A hint of a smile played around Prilla's lips, and Carol's own tense muscles relaxed as she remembered the odd little lady and her cheerful, whimsical home.

"But Blanche—you know she's a bit senile, the poor dear—kept mixing up my father with the ghost and faerie stories she'd heard." Prilla shook her head. "I didn't want to leave her upset, but I couldn't stay to calm her down."

"Understandable," the chief said.

"On another trip to town, I checked on my cabin. It was still a disaster area." Prilla's nose wrinkled at the memory. "I wanted to clean up the mess Kristen made, but he would have asked me lots of questions if I came back from town late." She stiffened slightly, her hands clenching. "At first, I was just mad that Kristen didn't pick up after herself. The next time I stopped there, though, I realized she'd left without telling me. I wasn't really surprised. But Kristen hadn't taken her clothes or makeup with her, and that was strange."

Harvey and Carol exchanged fretful glances.

"I knew then that something bad had happened to her," Prilla went on. "And though my father wouldn't talk about Kristen, I heard people at the grocery store saying she'd been found dead." Though shaking all over, Prilla faced Chief Thomson, unblinking. "I confronted my father about her death, and he wouldn't say a word. Not at the time anyway."

"Did he eventually tell you anything?" the chief asked.

"Yes, he told me when he picked me up outside Kristen's funeral." Tears welled in Prilla's eyes.

"You brought her flowers, didn't you?" Carol asked.

"I did. Though we fought a lot, she's the only sister I ever had. I wanted to say goodbye, but I was afraid the police would find me, so I just left the flowers."

"Actually, the police found your pickup halfway to Marquette," Carol said. "Did you walk all that way?"

"No." Prilla shook her head. "A lady truck driver saw me get out of my pickup and offered me a ride. She was very nice."

Thank goodness for that guardian angel on wheels. "But your father was there," Carol prompted.

"Yes. He must have been watching for me near the funeral home and followed me. When I walked to an all-night store and bought a doughnut for breakfast, he came in and bought one too. He took me out to his car, where he said the police were looking for me." Her gaze moved to the chief. "That they were sure I was the one who'd killed Kristen, and he wanted to help me get away to Canada."

"We had no proof that you'd done it," Thomson said, "but in a murder case, a close relative usually is considered a person of interest. Especially if that relative disappears."

"I understand." Prilla wrung her hands. "But now I know he wasn't trying to protect me. He wanted to keep me away from the police so I couldn't tell them where he was."

"Because he killed Kristen?" Carol said.

"No, because he was still on the run from that insurance scam." Prilla took a deep breath. "He told me that Kristen had contacted one of his victims and convinced him to pay her to set up a meeting in Faerie Copse the night she died. She lured my father there so the guy could—I don't know what, really, but I think he wanted revenge rather than for my father to go to jail. But my father waited just outside the copse to watch, because he guessed it was a trap. After a while, the guy started getting antsy because my father was late, and he got mad at Kristen because he thought she'd stolen his money too. He lost his temper and killed her with the knife she'd brought along for that awful prank. My father said he couldn't do anything for her and didn't want the same thing to happen to him, so he ran."

Carol's mind reeled with this drastic turn of events. She'd been convinced that Nilson had killed Kristen, as horrifying as the idea was. Then again, it was possible Nilson was telling tales to cover himself. But now there was another suspect, another lead for Chief Thomson to chase.

"You mentioned the name Bryan Strong," the chief said. "Is that the guy your father saw kill Kristen?"

"Yes," Prilla confirmed.

"We'll follow up on it." He jotted down the name. "Nilson told us a similar story, though we weren't ready to believe him just yet."

"I wasn't ready to believe him either, but I didn't have any other choice," Prilla said. "He told me that even though he knew who killed Kristen, I was still in danger, and that if he got caught for the insurance scam, he wouldn't be able to help me. He said we'd hide out at the lighthouse again until he could figure out what to do. I hated that place, but I agreed anyway." Her lower lip trembled. "He kept reminding me he was the only family I had left."

Carol's stomach rolled at the havoc Nilson had wreaked on his daughter's good heart.

"After we came back from Marquette, he wouldn't let me go anywhere," Prilla continued. "He sneaked into town in the middle of the night and broke into The Hamper to get supplies. Otherwise, we wouldn't have had anything to eat."

"So you were there the day before yesterday," Carol murmured. "My friends and I came looking for you that day. Did you see us? We were trying to stay hidden—"

"I didn't see anything." Prilla's eyes widened. "He'd ordered me to lie on the floor and not move. By the time he let me stand up, it was night. Then the next morning, he said he'd finally figured out how to get us to Canada. He made me call you and lure you to us, and then he dragged us out in front of all those people."

"Oh Prilla," Carol said, squeezing her friend's hand.

Prilla's shoulders shook. "When he first talked me into going to the lighthouse, he said we'd have a whole new life together in Canada. I tried to believe him." She gritted her teeth. "What was I thinking? He never meant for me to go with him. He would have left me behind. Or worse."

Carol's heart broke for her friend. Then she remembered that she'd asked Chief Thomson to bring something to the interview.

He seemed to have remembered too. The chief removed a small, plastic evidence bag from his desk drawer and handed it to Prilla. "I believe this belongs to you."

A hesitant smile playing on her lips, Prilla peered into the bag, and tears spilled down her face. "My locket! I thought it was gone. Where did you find it?"

Carol hated to answer, but she told the truth. "In Kristen's backpack."

Prilla nodded, as if she'd known all along. "Am I allowed to hold it?"

"Sure," the chief answered. "We've already done all the tests we'll do."

Prilla removed the locket from the bag and dangled it in front of her face. The pendant glimmered in the office lighting as it swayed back and forth on its chain. The lines of pain in her face softened.

"I wish we could let you take it home now," the chief said. "But when all this is resolved, we'll make sure you get it back."

"That helps." Prilla reluctantly replaced the locket in the bag. "I wondered if Kristen had taken it, but with all her flashy clothes, I couldn't believe she'd want it. And with them already fighting all the time, I guess I didn't want to make things worse." Her head bowed again. "Besides, I couldn't stand to think she'd take Mom's locket from me."

Carol boiled inside. The two had different mothers. Why had Kristen stolen something that meant everything to Prilla and absolutely nothing to her? *She probably meant to pawn it. Or she was just being awful because she could.*

"But maybe she was jealous," Prilla murmured thoughtfully. "She'd stayed with us. She knew my mom loved me. Maybe Kristen wished her mom had given her something special too."

Carol placed a reassuring arm around Prilla's shoulders and gave her a squeeze. "Chief, can Prilla take the locket today? You said you were done testing it, and it's all she has from her mom. I'm sure she'd be happy to allow you access if you find you need it again in your investigation."

"Oh I would!" Prilla said eagerly.

"Still interfering, Carol?" the chief asked, but his words held more amusement than reproach. He waved at the bag. "Go ahead, Prilla. You've more than earned it with all your help in capturing Nilson and telling me everything."

Prilla clutched the locket as if it were her last lifeline, her eyes shining. "Thank you so much. You have no idea what this means to me. And I'll tell you anything else you want to know."

"There's a lot more to cover, but I think we should take a break until Monday," the chief said. "After what you've all been through, that's enough for one day. And I have a lead to follow up on. You go get some rest."

Carol, Harvey, and Prilla left town hall and headed home for an early supper and early bedtime. The ride was nearly silent, each passenger weary and thoughtful as Harvey drove them back into the woods.

Prilla would spend at least another night in the guest room—and as far as Carol was concerned, as many nights as she needed until she felt comfortable going back to her own cabin.

Long after saying good night to her friend and climbing into her own bed, however, Carol still lay awake, worrying about Prilla and wondering what it would take for her to get over the trauma of the past few days, not to mention her sister's death. *A good support system for a start,* Carol told herself. *And that's exactly what she has now.*

18

After all the guns, fears, and tears—oh the joy of frosting a teddy bear cake for a two-year-old's birthday party. Despite occasional tight deadlines, Carol had always enjoyed decorating cakes. That Monday morning, though, with each row of chocolate frosting she piped, a tiny spot in her soul mended. "It's so good to be back at work," she announced as she finished filling in a paw.

"It's so good to have you." Laura, drizzling chocolate cobwebs onto mini chocolate-pecan pies, threw Carol an ear-to-ear smile.

Carol paused to admire her partner's work. "Way to get into the Halloween spirit."

"Holiday stuff sells like hotcakes," Molly said brightly as she continued reloading Abernethy biscuits onto a tray destined for the display case. She looked up at Carol. "It's so great to see you smile."

"I can't tell you how wonderful it feels to be here." Carol knew she owed these friends so much. "I told you I was sorry for playing the Lone Ranger, for causing you both so much worry. But an apology seems so small. It's not enough."

"Yes, you have been a royal pain," Laura said with a wicked grin, then slyly exchanged glances with Molly. "But you're awfully good at decorating cakes, so we'll keep you around."

"Speaking of cakes," Molly said, then bit her lip. "Jenny called earlier to say she's stopping by soon with the supplies for her friends' wedding cake."

"Supplies?" Carol's eyebrow shot up. She immediately felt a wave of dread. She'd nearly forgotten about Sophia and Elijah's special request. "You mean the . . ."

"Adorable, precious fish?" Jenny finished from the doorway. She held a cardboard box in her hands. "Never you fear. They're right here."

Carol suppressed a groan. *The customer is always right,* she reminded herself. "Well, bring it over to the surface farthest from our work spaces." She gestured for Jenny to follow to the table where they packed their Internet orders for shipment.

With a surprising lack of grace, Jenny dropped the box on the table with a thud. "That was getting heavy," she said, adjusting the fabric headband that held her natural curls at bay.

"You could have been a little more careful with live creatures," Carol chided her daughter.

"I didn't think you were too wild about this idea in the first place," Jenny replied. "Maybe I just did you a favor."

"Jennifer Felicia MacCallan, you watch yourself." Invoking Jenny's maiden name to show she meant business, Carol shot her daughter a stern frown. "Do you know how much trouble I'd be in for killing these fish?" Out of the corner of her eye, she noticed that the top flap of the box was twitching. "What on earth?"

In horror, Carol watched as white foam burst forth from the box. Two red fish rode the wave, and she shrieked as they fell to the floor.

Carol stared at the mess, slowly registering what she was looking at. Her expression of horror transformed quickly into fury as she realized that what she'd thought were Romeo and Juliet the goldfish were actually gummy candies. "Jennifer . . ." she growled in a warning tone.

Jenny crossed her arms and smirked. "What?"

After another glare at her daughter, Carol poked the box's flaps tentatively, wary of more hijinks, then lifted one flap. On its underside was a single word scrawled in thick, black marker. *Gotcha!*

Jenny, Molly, and Laura burst into fits of laughter. Molly even pulled out her phone to take photos of Carol's reaction to the prank.

"Very funny," Carol growled, grabbing the closest towel to mop up the quickly deflating foam. "I'm so glad I wrote those checks for your degree in chemistry so you could repay me so kindly with this demonstration of your knowledge."

Jenny's laughter finally petered out, and she accepted a towel from Laura to help with the cleanup. "Come on, Mom. It's the Month of the Faeries. You didn't think I'd let you off, did you?"

"I thought you said you didn't approve of the shenanigans," Carol said.

"I don't," Jenny agreed. "But I also don't approve of you almost getting yourself killed, and look how that turned out."

Carol set aside her towel and pulled her daughter into a tight hug. "I'm sorry I scared you," she murmured into her daughter's ear. "That was never my intention."

"No," Jenny said, returning the embrace. "You were just doing the right thing. I can't fault you for that."

"No, but you did punish me for it with your little stunt." Carol pulled back and frowned at the box. "So do you know when the real fish are coming?"

Jenny giggled again, then it turned into a full-blown belly laugh. When she finally came up for air, she gasped, "Oh, Mom. There are no fish. Sophia and Elijah aren't crazy . . . just up for a good prank. They couldn't wait to help me celebrate your first Month of the Faeries."

"Oh, you!" Carol grabbed the towel and flicked it at her daughter, who quickly sidestepped it.

"Don't be mad at them, though," Jenny said. "I promised I'd take the heat and make sure you knew in plenty of time that they want real cake—not an aquarium—for all four tiers of their cake."

Carol managed a smile. "That's a relief, I don't mind telling you."

"What in heaven is all the fuss in here?" Hamish demanded as he entered the kitchen.

"Jenny just helped Carol celebrate the Month of the Faeries," Laura said.

"A suitable justice for the worry she caused us all, I'm sure." Hamish's gaze settled on Molly. "Just desserts come to all in good time." He turned on his heel and left the kitchen as quickly as he'd come in.

Molly froze, her face a mask of fear. Then she slapped her forehead. "He's still going to get me. I thought he'd forgotten. It's been *weeks*."

"The Seven Days of Kindness are coming," Carol said. "Only a few more days before Hamish has to cease and desist. Maybe if we keep him extra busy, he won't have time—"

"Oh, he'll manage, no matter what to-do list we throw at him." Molly grimaced. "Even if he plays his little trick at two minutes till midnight on Halloween."

"Maybe we could bribe Joyce to keep him at home," Laura suggested. "Stay strong, Molly."

Carol was about to chime in with more support when a bell sounded in her brain. The name of the man Nilson had said killed Kristen was Bryan Strong. *Is there any chance . . . ?*

Struck by a hunch, Carol pulled out her phone and searched *Bryan Strong Detroit* in the browser. A moment later, a list of news article links appeared. She clicked one and skimmed the story, which identified Bryan Strong as a victim of the insurance scam perpetrated by Marshall Hale—Nilson's alias. She went back to the results list and clicked on a link to a social media page. When it came up, a familiar face stared back from its profile photo. "It's the potbellied man from the funeral," she murmured, barely believing it. "I wonder if he went there hoping to find Nilson."

Jenny raised an eyebrow. "What's that, Mom?"

"Can you excuse me for a moment?" Carol asked. "I need to make a call."

"No problem. We can talk later." Jenny waved Carol off, then went to work cleaning up the rest of her prank's mess. Carol went into the quiet storeroom and called the chief to share her discovery.

"I was just about to call you, Carol," Chief Thomson said. "As it turns out, Bryan Strong—"

"Really did kill Kristen?" Carol finished. "He's the guy I saw at the funeral. The one I thought was a reporter or a plainclothes policeman."

"Yes, I know."

"You do?" Carol was confused.

"I was literally on the phone with a detective in the Detroit Police Department when Mr. Strong walked into the station to confess. He said he couldn't spend another day with it on his conscience."

"So he corroborated Nilson's story?"

"Every detail. And he admitted that he'd gone to the funeral in the hopes that Nilson would be there and he could finally get his revenge. But after he went home, he thought about all the mourners there, and about what the pastor had said. He knew he had to confess to keep from going mad."

"Wow." Carol shook her head. "I can't believe it."

"I've had a hard time too, believe me." The chief chuckled drily. "To be honest, I think I'm most surprised that Nilson was actually telling the truth for once."

"No kidding," Carol agreed. "So do you still want us to come in today, or are you too busy wrapping up the case?"

"Actually, it's not the only case we're wrapping up," the chief said. "In addition to needing more details from Prilla, I also have much more to share with her. I thought I'd tell you first so you can digest the information a little before you have to help Prilla get a handle on it."

"All right," Carol said tentatively.

"Remember the knife from the Matt Boersma murder? The one that hadn't been tested for DNA by the sheriff?"

She'd almost forgotten. "The results came through?"

"Loud and clear." Instead of excited, the chief sounded almost sad, and Carol wondered what prompted it. "They found Kristen's DNA on that knife."

"You mean . . ." Carol choked on her words.

"Yes," Chief Thomson said, "we have every reason to believe that twenty-five years ago, Kristen Reed killed her sister's boyfriend."

The chief drummed his fingers on his desk, clearly hesitant.

Concerned about Prilla's pinched face, Carol reached over and grasped her hand. Prilla's other hand clutched the locket around her neck.

He began by confirming the circumstances of Kristen's death. Then, gently, he told Prilla that her sister not only had been murdered, but probably had been a murderer herself.

Prilla closed her eyes, absorbing the news. Tears streamed down her cheeks, then she lifted her gaze to the chief. "I always suspected it, but never had any proof. And I was afraid of her revenge if I told anyone."

"You can tell me now," the chief said.

Prilla inhaled. "Back in high school, she told me she couldn't understand what Matt ever saw in me, then she made a play for him. Granted, Kristen made a play for every guy she met." She gripped the locket. "I always assumed he rejected her, and she got really, really mad."

"Do you have any idea why Kristen painted that Celtic symbol on Boersma's face?" Chief Thomson asked.

"Kristen knew Mom and I liked Celtic stories and symbols and things. Kristen teased me about it mercilessly in front of other kids."

Carol felt a surge of anger. Kristen had been a bully, and Prilla had deserved better.

"I'm sure she painted that on Matt with my charcoal," Prilla continued, "hoping the police would connect it to me. One more thing to make them think I killed him."

Carol tried to think of something comforting to say, but couldn't. Chief Thomson remained silent.

Finally, without raising her eyes, Prilla asked, "How is my dad?"

"Out of the hospital with a clean bill of health and in jail, where he'll stay for a good long time," the chief answered. "He gave up the account number for the bank where he stashed the insurance fraud money, hoping for leniency. I doubt he'll get that, but at least his victims will get their money back."

Prilla didn't respond to this information, but Carol saw that her eyes were troubled once more. "If it's all right with you," she told Thomson, "I'm going to take Prilla back to my house for some rest."

With a glance at Prilla's face, the chief agreed.

As soon as they got home, Prilla fell into a deep sleep. Carol and Harvey didn't hear a peep from her all evening. While Carol stared at the ceiling again instead of sleeping, Prilla apparently slept all night and was still slumbering when Carol left for work.

She didn't mind that business was slow at the bakery that morning. Laura sequestered herself in a kitchen corner to research the latest culinary trends while Carol, Molly, and Fergus sat around a table by the fireplace to drink coffee and chat in between customers.

A couple eating scones still lingered at the table nearest the door, so Carol lowered her voice. "Prilla handled the whole thing better than I thought. Better than I did, actually."

"She doesn't look like it, but that woman must be made of steel," Molly said. "But I'm glad to hear she's going to seek out counseling so she can heal."

"It's just awful that her father played on her tendency to see the best in people," Carol said. "She deserved a much better family than the one she got."

Molly and Fergus agreed.

Wanting a break from the topic, Carol grabbed the chance to steer their conversation away from Prilla's struggles. "Speaking of dads, how's yours, Fergus?"

"Still a bit ornery," Fergus confessed, then shrugged. "Perhaps with the resolution of all this brouhaha, he'll settle down and go to Arizona."

"In the meantime, we should be thinking of ways to celebrate the end of murder and mayhem," Molly said brightly.

"And the end of the Month of the Faeries," Fergus said, nudging her with a grin.

"That too." Molly sighed. "I'm still waiting for Hamish's ax to fall. But after all this, maybe that's not such a big deal."

"Perhaps we could celebrate by doing something special for Prilla," Carol said. "Something fun and helpful. Let's do it during the Seven Days of Kindness."

"Love it!" Molly the event planner forgot about doom and gloom. They tossed ideas back and forth until two more customers entered, and Molly headed for the counter to wait on them.

"As much as I enjoy your company, I'd better get back to the resort," Fergus said as he got up from his chair.

"Same here." Carol stood. "I still need to frost a few gazillion cookies for us to hand out during Loch Mallaig's downtown trick-or-treating tomorrow night."

Fergus was about to say something else, but his phone started ringing. He pulled it out of his pocket and frowned at the screen, then answered with a terse, "Hello?"

Sensing trouble, perhaps with his father again, Carol was torn between supporting her friend and giving him space. Before she could decide, however, Fergus had ended his call and was staring at Carol, a perplexed expression on his face.

"Is something wrong?" Carol asked.

"That was Wilma Guthrie," Fergus said, bewilderment coloring his tone. "Dad's at police headquarters."

"Oh no! Is he okay?"

"He doesn't appear to be sick. But he's saying weird things, like he shouldn't have kept quiet about Matt Boersma's murder." Fergus shook his head. "Something's very, very wrong."

19

Although Prilla was a homebody, Carol and Harvey convinced her to come out to dinner with them at Neeps and Tatties that evening. As they devoured Caboc cheese on oatcakes and hearty Cullen skink—a smoked-fish stew—Carol and Harvey learned their friend had eaten there only once, on her birthday years before.

Reminded of poor Birdie, who hadn't had two pennies to rub together thanks to her leech of a boyfriend, Carol resolved more than ever to make good things happen for Prilla. The Seven Days of Kindness should only be a start.

They were just finishing after-dinner coffee when Carol answered a call from Fergus. Perhaps now they'd find out how Gordon was doing—and what had prompted his visit to the police.

Instead, Fergus asked with little prelude, "Carol, will you bring Prilla to Castleglen? Dad told Chief Thomson a story he thinks Prilla should hear," Fergus explained. "A story that explains why Matt Boersma's murder went unsolved for so many years."

Carol exhaled. Hadn't her friend experienced enough surprises the past few days?

Though Fergus didn't press her, she sensed how important this was to Gordon. "I'll check with Prilla, then call you back."

When Carol asked about the meeting, Prilla stared. "I've never met him. Why would he want to talk with me?"

Reluctantly, Carol echoed Fergus's explanation. She added, "These days, Gordon seems easily upset. What he has to say might sound a little odd."

"But Fergus helped you look for me, didn't he?" At Carol's assent, Prilla lifted her chin. "I might not be able to help his dad or answer his questions, but I'm glad to try." Her voice wobbled a little. "Would you stay with me while we talk?"

"Of course," Carol reassured her, then called Fergus back to say they were on their way.

Carol had had enough excitement, and she imagined Harvey had too. But they drove to Castleglen anyway as the sun faded in the sky, hoping that Prilla wouldn't suffer any more trauma. Afterward, they could go home, cozy up, and warm their feet in front of the fireplace.

The fireplace fantasy, at least, came true at Castleglen. Fergus showed them to a small, luxurious den near his office, where cushy leather sofas surrounded a crackling fire. Through the wall-size windows, lights from a few boats on Loch Mallaig and the lake's opposite shore twinkled through the twilight.

"Dad's refuge before he retired," Fergus said as they entered the room. "Works for me too."

At their approach, Gordon stood to welcome them. "Come in, come in." He extended his hand to Prilla and introduced himself. "Thanks so much for coming. I know you've had a horrible time lately."

With his gracious greeting, Carol relaxed. This was the Gordon she remembered.

An awkward silence fell when they all sat down. Finally Gordon said, "There's no easy way to introduce this, so I'm just going to dive in."

Prilla's fingers dug into the sofa's arm.

"This concerns the death of Matt Boersma twenty-five years ago," Gordon continued. "I understand he was your friend at the time?"

"Yes," Prilla answered. "We were dating."

Gordon winced. "I'm sorry to bring up sad memories."

"It was a long time ago." Prilla spoke in a soft but steady voice.

Gordon cleared his throat. "Yes it was. The sheriff then, Don Lawrence, was a close friend of mine. He was a good man, and he cared very much about Loch Mallaig and its people. But he was a man, and he—well, he made mistakes like everyone else."

What in the world? Carol realized she, Harvey, and Prilla had all leaned forward in their seats.

Gordon went on. "He investigated the Boersma murder, of course, but they never found out who committed it. He and his officers did discover the murder weapon, a knife, buried near Boersma's body. It had been wiped clean, except for a messy, partial fingerprint or two that led nowhere. Until . . ." He paused.

"You mean until the police found out my sister killed Matt?" Prilla's voice shook a little, but she didn't shrink away.

Gordon nodded. "Until now, everyone believed Sheriff Lawrence had done all he could, that the case was legitimately unsolved. But several years after the murder, I found out differently." He paused before going on. "Don had learned he had terminal cancer. Before he died, he told me something he'd never told anyone else, not even his wife or kids. Something he regretted very much." Now his voice trembled. He glanced toward Prilla. "I hate to say this, but since you were suspected and since you were close to Matt, I feel you have the right to know."

"Go on." Prilla sounded stronger than Gordon.

"Well, you probably knew that Matt dated lots of girls."

"Yes."

Gordon cleared his throat. "Among them was Stella, the daughter of Don's brother, Randy. He hated Matt Boersma because he believed he'd ruined Stella's reputation. Randy had even run him off his property a time or two. When Boersma turned up dead, Don was sure his brother had killed him, even though he denied it vehemently. So Don couldn't bring himself to do the DNA testing. In his public statement, he said that the fingerprints were inconclusive, which was true. Nobody questioned his judgment, especially since DNA evidence wasn't as mainstream an idea as it is now. Lots of people—including other angry fathers whose daughters Matt led astray—weren't too upset at his death. But Don suffered extreme guilt all those years. He told me what he'd done only two days before he died."

Gordon hung his head as if to compose himself. Fergus pressed his father's shoulder.

Carol glanced sideways at Prilla, whose face remained blank as she waited for the rest of Gordon's story.

"When the papers brought up the Boersma case again," Gordon finally continued, "I thought for sure someone would find out Don had suppressed evidence. That his reputation and his family, who still live in Loch Mallaig, would be dragged through the mud. His brother's name too—though he's dead as well. But Stella's married and still lives around here. She has four children, Randy's grandchildren. I'm close to that family." His shoulders sagged. "I couldn't stand the thought that through no fault of their own they'd bear the impact of his wrongdoing, long after his death."

Carol's heart went out to the man who had guarded his dead friend's secret for so many years. Yet Prilla had suffered suspicion—had even been jailed—because Sheriff Lawrence had prioritized his family. Because that case had never been solved, suspicion of Prilla had resurfaced. Was that injustice—along with her father's betrayal and the crushing new knowledge that her sister had murdered Matt—going to be the straw that broke Prilla's back?

Carol took her hand, but Prilla didn't squeeze back. Instead, the quiet woman leveled a hard gaze at Gordon. "I wish Sheriff Lawrence had told the truth. That you had told what you knew."

"I do too," Gordon murmured.

"I wish we all had told the truth," Prilla said, her voice growing more forceful. "I wish Kristen had told the truth about trying to take my boyfriend and stealing my locket. I wish my father hadn't pretended he cared about us. I wish his actions hadn't compelled an otherwise good man to murder Kristen." Her eyes blazed blue fire. "I wish I'd told myself the truth, that my father is a bad man who cares only about himself." She turned to Carol. "I lied to you, a friend I didn't deserve, and put you in danger."

Carol started to respond, but no words came out.

"I covered for my father again and again," Prilla said, her gaze sweeping everyone in the room. "I shouldn't have done that. I should have gone to the police." Tears rolling down her face, she held out her hand to Gordon. "Thank you for telling me the truth. I'm sorry for all those years you covered up for your friend. That you worried for nothing."

Gordon patted her hand. "We all make mistakes."

"I suppose there's one more thing I should tell the truth about." Prilla shifted in her seat to face Carol. "Do you remember when I told you how my father knew about the lighthouse? That Grandpa had hidden things he stole there?"

Carol furrowed her brow, wondering what that could possibly have to do with anything. "Yes, I think so."

Prilla took a deep breath. "He also told me that a long time ago, when Grandpa was hiding there, some teen boys came snooping around. When one climbed the inside stairs to the top, Grandpa sneaked up on him and pushed him out the window."

Carol gasped. After all the events of the past month, she had thought nothing could shock her. She'd been wrong.

"I didn't tell Chief Thomson about Grandpa because I figured there was nothing he could do about it now. But I'm done covering for my family, and that boy's family deserves to know what really happened to him." Prilla stood. "If you don't mind, I'd like to go tell Chief Thomson about it as soon as possible."

———————— ❈ ————————

How could mere days make such a difference in a person?

Less than forty-eight hours earlier, Carol had witnessed Prilla's wrenching final revelations. Today, she marveled at her friend's expression of quiet contentment as she arranged jack-o'-lantern, ghost, and black cat cookies with sliced apples on trays in the bakehouse kitchen. She even hummed occasionally as she worked. While Carol and her partners baked and frosted the last batches of Halloween cookies, Prilla cleared prep tables, washed dishes and pans, and swept floors.

That evening, she beamed as she showed off the costume Carol, Molly, and Laura had hurriedly concocted for her. Her blonde hair twisted into braids, Prilla wore her own long skirt, a ruffled white top on loan from Carol, and a bakehouse white apron. They also borrowed a shepherd's crook from the church's Christmas pageant costume closet, and Maisie graciously furnished Prilla with an oversize stuffed lamb from her burgeoning toy collection. With blue satin ribbons, a few added lacy frills, and new color in her cheeks, Prilla resembled a nursery rhyme picture of Mary and her little lamb.

Hamish and Joyce wore Bruce plaids with masquerade masks. From time to time, their disguises made Carol do a double take, wondering who these mysterious people were. Hamish occasionally brandished his plastic sword à la Robert the Bruce so everyone would know who was really in charge.

Laura had dusted off some roller skates she'd found in her parents' basement on her last visit and was dressed as a bad-to-the-bone roller derby girl, black rectangles painted beneath her eyes and all. The most athletic of the bunch, she skated from kitchen to customer area with grace and ease.

Harvey had insisted he would only wear his fisherman's garb, so Carol concocted a fish costume from a sparkly shower curtain she'd bought at a secondhand store.

She and Prilla added a few final decorations to those remaining from the Harvest Party. As they lit candles in the darkened eating area and on the front porch, Prilla said, "This is so fun. I haven't been to a party in years."

"I hadn't really thought of it as a party," Carol said. "Just a nice way to give a break to families who are trick-or-treating. The kids will like it, and after walking around town, parents are ready to sit and relax."

"It's a party to me." Prilla's face took on the candles' glow as she moved to her position behind the counter with the Bruces, where she would help serve.

Molly, wearing a darling white cat costume, stopped under the pretense of finalizing a few details with Carol. Her whiskers waggled as she sent a pointed look at the coffee bar, where Hamish was helping Joyce set up. "Look at him. So innocent, so helpful. Hamish still has six hours before midnight and the beginning of the Seven Days of Kindness. Who knows when he'll pull something on me tonight, right in front of the whole town? I wish—"

Enough of this prank business. "I wish you'd just go and ask him what meanness he has in mind," Carol urged. "Maybe that will take the fun out, and he'll decide to forget it. You'll both be done with this silly game."

"Easy for you to say," Molly retorted. "He targeted you early. One dumb rubber snake, and it was over."

"Yeah, loved the snake." Recalling Harvey's panic, she rolled her eyes. "Easy."

Molly grinned at Carol, then quickly closed the short distance between herself and the Bruces. "All right, Hamish. Spill it," she demanded, though her fuzzy costume somewhat diluted her attempt to sound stern.

He leaned on his sword and put on a heavy Scottish brogue. "I cannae imagine what you're blethering on about."

"Yes you can." Molly scowled. "You've waited all month to get your revenge on me. Just do it. Now."

"I have no intention of getting revenge, as you call it. True, I served justice to your coconspirators, and that obligated me to treat you all equally."

"And?" Molly prompted.

Hamish adopted a thoughtful expression. "The truth is, no matter how I tried, I could not conceive of a better prank than Fergus's. So I simply did nothing at all."

Molly gaped at him.

"You certainly cannae accuse me of wrongdoing," Hamish continued. "You let your imagination run away with all sorts of wicked ideas, and you've been paranoid all month for nothing." He shook his finger at Molly. "You did all the work for me." He walked away, whistling.

Molly stood frozen for a few moments, then her hands flew up to cover her face, and she began making noises Carol had never heard her friend make before.

Concerned for Molly, Carol patted her back gently. "There, there. Don't take it too hard."

"Too hard?" Molly ceased her screeching and moved her hands to reveal an ear-to-ear grin. Apparently she'd been laughing. "He got me good. No arguing that."

Relieved that Molly had accepted the news of Hamish's punishment with good grace, Carol settled into enjoying what turned out to be a raucous, joyful, and very busy evening. Their visitor tally topped all expectations, which kept everyone smiling and running. For several hours, they served refreshments, admired costumes, and chatted with grateful parents who wanted to thaw their feet in front of the fire. Prilla, Carol noted, had appeared a little overwhelmed by the noisy crowd. No wonder, after having been isolated in that cabin for so long. But she'd smiled shyly when little ones wanted to pet her lamb and had even mimicked sheep noises for them, much to their delight.

Carol was just returning from the kitchen with their last tray of cookies when Chief Thomson stepped through the front door with two youngsters dressed as superheroes. His own two daughters, Lindsay and Kay, were in college, so Carol guessed these kids were extended relatives or kids of friends. She bustled forward to greet them.

"These are my neighbors, Jackson and Mia," the chief said. "Kids, this is Mrs. MacCallan." After the children offered polite greetings, Thomson continued, "Their mom wasn't feeling well tonight, so they're helping me on Halloween patrol. Though I think they're taking candy bribes." He eyed them suspiciously, making them giggle.

"Crime won't stand a chance against you three," Carol said with a smile. "Want to power up with a cookie?"

"Yes please!" the siblings chorused.

After the kids ate, they went outdoors to play with Angus, who sported a bright orange sweater with a jack-o'-lantern face on it for the occasion.

As they watched through the window, Carol said to the chief, "I hope things quiet down a bit for you. Solving two murders in a week must have put quite a strain on your staff."

"All in a day's work," Thomson said. "Besides, we had you doing all the heavy lifting."

Carol chuckled. "I'd say anytime, but I hope to never find myself in a situation like that again."

"Still, Prilla has you to thank for bringing her home safely." Thomson shifted his attention to the café area, where Prilla was gathering used napkins and cups and washing empty tables, a placid smile across her face. "She's lucky to have a friend like you."

"No," Carol said, remembering how Prilla had swung the chain at her father's knees to save Carol's life. "I'm the lucky one."

That Sunday, after attending service at St. Andrews Church and enjoying Reverend Findlay's sermon about kindness and generosity—a thinly veiled lecture for those who had participated in the Month of the Faeries—Carol was glad to finally let her body get some much-needed rest after nonstop excitement.

"Since when did refilling my coffee cup turn into an Olympic event?" Carol gestured to her empty mug, which she was too tired to top off, as they watched a steady rain patter against the living room window. "Even breathing seems like work."

"You sit." Harvey handled the task for her, pouring himself a warm-up while he was at it. "Go against your usual inclinations and try to stay still for a few hours. Anything more strenuous than turning a page or pressing a button is strictly forbidden."

"Works for me." Carol picked up the book she'd been trying to read for a month and snuggled close to Harvey as he paged through a magazine.

By nightfall, she'd summoned enough energy to check her e-mail. When she pulled up her social media page, she gasped. She had a friend request from Julia Birdie Henson.

Julia? That was Birdie's first name? The surname Henson didn't ring any bells. She must have married someone other than that awful man she'd been with back when Carol had known her.

Heart fluttering like a sparrow's wings, Carol read the accompanying message.

> *Hi Carol, I saw your name in a newspaper article this week and wasn't surprised to read that you were a local hero. Do you remember me from our teaching days in Pittsburgh? I've never forgotten your kindness, the one bright spot then. I would love to catch up with you if you have time.*

Carol clicked the link to Birdie's profile page. Her photo brought a smile. The once colorless, drained woman now beamed next to a portly, bearded man who gazed at her with utter adoration in his eyes. Definitely an upgrade.

As she scrolled down the page and admired family photos showing children and grandchildren, a prayer of Thanksgiving swelled in Carol's heart. She accepted the friend request and wrote, *I can't tell you how many times I've thought of you . . .*

"My cabin's going to be beautiful." Prilla clasped her hands as she glanced around her home, which she'd clearly missed.

"Thank goodness the police finally finished their investigation," Carol said, then regretted she'd even mentioned them.

Prilla, however, was making good on her vow to forget the past and invest in her future. As Carol had thought, the Seven Days of Kindness that followed the Month of the Faeries had proven the perfect time to help Prilla reinvent herself. For starters, Prilla had welcomed Carol's and Laura's invitation to their Fair Knitting Ladies meeting. To their surprise, she'd also attended a church choir rehearsal, and Molly had reported that she had a beautiful voice. And Doreen Giobsan had offered to hire Prilla as a part-time employee for the holidays, insisting that introducing her customers to the artist who created those beautiful woodland and Celtic carvings would boost sales.

Now, on the seventh Day of Kindness, Fergus, Harvey, and Hamish had joined forces to repair Prilla's leaking roof and deteriorating windows while Laura, Molly, and Carol took her shopping for a new bed and bright-colored linens, as well as a new outfit, including fashionable boots to replace the clumpy old ones.

After they hung freshly ironed curtains at the cabin's windows, Prilla thanked them all for their generosity and gave them a picture she had designed. The wood-burned design depicted a still life of a loaf of bread, a cupcake, and a bap entwined with Celtic knots.

Carol, Molly, and Laura exclaimed over her thank-you gift.

"Let's hang it in the bakehouse dining area," Carol said, to which her partners enthusiastically agreed. "And we'll tell everyone who asks about it where they can get their own beautiful artwork."

Prilla threw her arms around Carol and hugged her tightly. "You are the best friend a girl could ask for."

A knock on the door interrupted their celebration, and Prilla opened it to find a beaming Blanche, wearing her signature red scarf and holding out a big bouquet of bittersweet berries.

Prilla welcomed her with a hug. After calling to the guys on the roof to come down for a coffee break, she packed a bag of groceries for Blanche and set it near the door so she'd remember it on her way out.

Once she'd handed Blanche a mug of coffee and seated her near the fireplace to thaw out, Prilla turned to Carol and her partners. "Did you know Blanche can knit? She made that beautiful red scarf."

"Then you really should come with us to the Fair Knitting Ladies meeting on Thursday night," Laura said to Blanche, who smiled demurely in response, her cheeks coloring.

The men entered then, cold, loud, and ready for a snack. Everyone drank coffee and cider and ate Joyce's delectable pumpkin spice doughnuts—all except Molly, for whom she'd baked a few plain ones.

The room rang with talk and laughter. The merriment waned a little, though, when Blanche began to wander around Prilla's cabin, checking behind the curtains and peering into cabinets.

"Can I help you find something, Blanche?" Carol asked, curious.

The peculiar little woman shook her head and continued her search. She insisted on seeing the loft and climbed the ladder with far more agility than Carol expected. Then she walked around the outside of the cabin.

Apparently satisfied, Blanche reentered and announced. "There aren't any cursed faeries in this house," she announced. "No ghosts."

"None at all," Prilla said with a smile.

"Only friends," Blanche confirmed, a grin lighting her little face.

"That's right," Carol agreed, mirroring the joyful expression along with the rest of her loved ones. "Only friends." And with friends like this, who could ask for anything more?